BOOKS BY SALLY M. RUSSELL

An Escape For Joanna
*Finding a Path to Happiness
*Dr. Wilder's Only True Love
*Josh and the Mysterious Princess
*A Summer's Adventure
A Surprise Awaits Back Home
#The Attorney and the Untamed Tigress
#Magic in the Bride's Bouquet
^Rewards of Faith

*Haven of Rest Ranch Series
#Sequel
^1st of a Sequel

REWARDS OF FAITH

SALLY M RUSSELL

WESTBOW
PRESS®
A DIVISION OF THOMAS NELSON
& ZONDERVAN

THE HOLY BIBLE, NEW INTERNATIONAL VERSION®, NIV® Copyright © 1973, 1978, 1984, 2011 by Biblica, Inc.® Used by permission. All rights reserved worldwide. Fiction disclaimer

WestBow Press books may be ordered through booksellers or by contacting:

WestBow Press
A Division of Thomas Nelson & Zondervan
1663 Liberty Drive
Bloomington, IN 47403
www.westbowpress.com
1 (866) 928-1240

ISBN: 978-1-5127-4746-1 (sc)
ISBN: 978-1-5127-4747-8 (e)

Print information available on the last page.

WestBow Press rev. date: 7/11/2016

This Book is Dedicated to the Memory of all those who influenced me as a teenager and all through my adult life to rely on my belief in God and to always have faith. They definitely made a big difference in my life.

She felt herself being held in the most
tender arms, but she couldn't open her
eyes.

"She's fainted," C.J. called to one of the bellhops
around the pool. "Please go and see if Emily can find
an extra room somewhere in the hotel." Carrying
Jessica in his arms as if she were a fragile doll, C.J.
also headed for the lobby. Everyone around the
pool turned to watch as the handsome owner of the
Beachside Resort carried his precious cargo.

> For I am the Lord, your God, who
> takes hold of your right hand and says
> to you, Do not fear, I will help you.
> Isaiah 41:13

CHAPTER ONE

Strolling along on the beautiful white sandy beach, Jessica was soon walking out in the water just far enough to keep her feet from burning on the hot sand. With her rather fair complexion, she had remembered to apply sunscreen and had grabbed her sunglasses and the wide brimmed hat that she'd bought especially for the beach, but her mind was otherwise so confused and heartbroken she hardly knew what was going on around her.

Yesterday, her world had seemed so complete. Now, as she splashed the water with each step she took, her mind was full of thoughts about this being her last year of college. In a couple more months she would receive a major in Education and also a minor in Business, and she hopes she'll be ready to pursue her dream. For years now she's been studying and working toward a position where she could teach in her own preschool to help little ones be ready to start kindergarten, and she'd thoroughly enjoyed the student teaching she'd done.

Of course, she'd always planned to work for a few years to accumulate the money to start her own school. Her family didn't have the money to help her in an endeavor that big, and the small jobs she'd had during her college years hadn't provided much for savings. She also had a small student loan to repay so she hoped she might get lucky enough to find a school already established that needed another teacher.

As she kept walking, she was also remembering how things had seemed to fall into place for her, especially when she thought back to when she'd met Todd Olsen just after the start of her junior year. *He'd wanted to start going steady almost immediately after our first date, but I understand all of that insistence a little bit better now. I'd told him that night that I'd never been with a man, and he'd been so excited about finding a virgin. After that, he'd become very protective and even tried to control most of my activities by always wanting to be with me if he wasn't with the team. I'd thought it was real sweet at the time but, oh how wrong I was.* She couldn't stop a few tears from running down her cheeks.

Todd had taken her to visit his parents several times. It was during one of those visits that his father had talked to her about her plans for teaching. He had even expressed a real interest in supporting her financially to get a school started.

She'd been so sure God had answered all of her prayers.

Well, she knew all that was certainly gone now. Todd had begged her for weeks to come to this Big Breaker Beach with him over spring break. She'd foolishly agreed when he'd promised to get a two-bedroom suite to appease her and her Christian beliefs. Over the past year and a half, she'd come to believe she could truly trust him. Even though he hadn't given her a ring, they had talked quite a bit about getting married after he'd gotten established in the business with his dad.

He was an only child, and she'd noticed that he was somewhat spoiled, an egotist, and possessive. He had even bragged about an outstanding job waiting for him right out of college. But, he'd also seemed quite mature in many ways, and he was looking forward to helping his dad increase their clientele. It was an architecture and design firm, employing approximately 30 full-time workers, and Todd had said he would get to start as one of two Vice-Presidents. He'd talked to her about how he'd like to do a lot of the traveling that his dad does for the business, because it could take him all over the world. She'd been very impressed but hadn't stopped to consider the problems all that traveling could possibly do to a marriage. With all the extensive travel he'd implied he wanted to do, would he ever be home to be a good father and husband?

Growing up with two sisters and in a small

town, she wasn't too familiar with boys and their expectations, and Todd had actually been her first serious boyfriend. She'd done mostly group dating, if that's what you want to call it, until she'd started college.

Everything had been fine until last night. After their arrival at the beach, they'd spent a little time playing volleyball with a group from school, and then they'd eaten a very delicious dinner in the hotel restaurant. He'd then suggested they go to their room and sit on the balcony where they could watch the waves break along the shore and the different type boats as they went sailing by. It had been so relaxing and he'd talked about owning a boat someday and his dreams of having a second home on one of the Carolina beaches.

But then, out of the blue, he'd gotten up and pulled her to her feet. Without a word, he'd quickly led her into the sitting room of their suite and started kissing and fondling her in ways he had never done before, and she noticed his breathing was heavy.

"Todd, what are you doing?" she'd asked as she'd pushed him away.

"I just feel I've waited long enough for you to get over your silly notion that sex is something you don't enjoy until after you're married, and I'm telling you right now, Jessica,

I plan to see that changed this week while we're here at the beach. We've been dating for a long time now, and if you love me like you say you do, you'll be willing to give me what I've been wanting for over a year."

She remembers every word during the argument that ensued. He'd informed her, in an arrogant way, that he'd been getting the satisfaction from other girls on campus that she hadn't been willing to give him. There were plenty who wanted to enjoy their college life by getting away from those dull studies and being with a man, but they weren't there for him tonight. With a big smirk on his face, he'd continued by saying that he was expecting to have his way with a virgin this time. "Just why do you think I've put up with your stupid beliefs for so long? I want a virgin, that's why!"

He had grabbed at her again but she'd given him a hard shove which had apparently surprised him and he'd landed on the floor. She'd been shocked, humiliated, and angered, but she'd still had time to quickly run to her room, slam the door shut and lock it before he could react. He'd then tried to sweet talk her back out by promising he would behave himself, he hadn't meant what he'd said, and she was the only one he'd ever cared for. She, of course, wasn't buying it. He'd finally grumbled something and she'd then heard a door slam. Since she wasn't sure if it was his room door or the suite door, she'd packed her bag, set the alarm and tried to rest until early in the morning when she thought he would surely be asleep. She'd then slipped out of the suite and hurried to the bus station, a few blocks away, just hoping she could catch a bus back to campus. Unfortunately, she discovered that the bus going toward Chapel Hill wouldn't be leaving until later in the day. She sat down on one of the benches in the station and tried to think what she should do.

She realized she had most of the day, so decided she might as well spend some more time on the beach. After all, that was what she'd come for, and she might possibly get her summer tan started. She put her bag in a locker at the station and then headed for the nice sandy beach. There were very few people around this early in the morning, but she knew she couldn't stay anywhere close because she couldn't let Todd find her.

She started to walk, not even sure or caring which direction she was going. It wasn't long before she'd noticed the sun was coming up on her left so she realized she was headed south. She then just kept walking and splashing the water with her feet as she went along. She even sat down a few times to try building a sand castle while mulling over the events of last night. *How could I have misjudged him so completely?*

She had no idea how long she'd been exposed to the sun, but she finally realized she was tired and getting a little weak. She'd also begun to feel really hungry and glanced at her watch. She couldn't believe it was almost 11 o'clock which meant she'd been on the beach over four hours. She remembered she'd left the hotel a little after 6 o'clock, but had been at the bus station for a little while before going to the beach. It also occurred to her, when she began to feel a little faint and nauseated, that she'd had nothing to eat except for a mint she'd found in her bag.

She looked around but nothing was familiar to her since she'd never been to this area before. She knew that she had passed several resorts and was now adjacent to another when her eyes started to get blurry and she'd really become frightened. She'd just decided she'd better sit down when she started slumping toward the sand, but she hadn't quite reached the ground when she felt herself being lifted and held in the most tender way, but she couldn't open her eyes or hear anything around her.

"She's fainted," C.J. called to one of the bellhops around the pool. "Please go and see if Emily can find an extra room somewhere in the hotel." Carrying Jessica in his arms as if she were a fragile doll, C.J. also headed for the lobby. Everyone on the beach and around the pool turned to watch as the handsome young owner of the Beachside Resort carried his precious cargo.

Emily was apologetic but not a single room was available. As C.J. motioned with his head, she hurried to open the door to his personal apartment and office. With Emily's help, he placed Jessica on the couch, removed her cap, and then they applied a cool cloth to her forehead. They carefully checked her small tote bag, hoping to find her name or some form of identification--possibly a close relative. They quickly discovered that her name is Jessica Lee Hale, her parents live in North Carolina, and that she's a senior this year and is attending UNC.

Their on-call physician, Dr. Chet Strom, came and checked her vitals. When he put a cold stethoscope on her chest, she jumped and opened her eyes. She was now really frightened because she didn't know where she was or who these people were. The doctor apologized for the cold shock he had given her, and the lady was smiling and asking if she could help her with anything. Just then she saw this tall handsome guy walking toward her carrying a glass of water, and the doctor began instructing her to sip the water a little at a time.

She didn't really want to stare, but for some reason she was sure she'd been close to this man before with his sandy-colored hair, beautiful brown eyes, and a gorgeous tan. In a nice pair of shorts and a snug fitting knit shirt, she could readily see an athletic build other men would die for. She quickly forced herself to look at the other two.

"What happened to me?" she whispered because her throat was too sore and dry to talk. She glanced around to see where she might be. "I remember walking for a long time and then feeling a little dizzy, but how did I get into this beautiful room?"

She tried to sit up but the doctor told her to lie still because she'd probably gotten overheated and would need to rest until her body could recover from the torture she'd put it through. He was smiling but continued with a soft, but scolding voice, "You really did punish yourself, you know."

"But," she whispered, "I don't know where I am and I don't know any of you."

"I'm Emily Brown," the lady spoke up. "This is C.J. Peterson, owner of Beachside Resort, and this is Dr. Chet Strom, the one who loves giving those cold shockers. Luckily, C.J. had been watching the activity on the beach and saw you as you were approaching the resort. He thought you appeared somewhat overcome by the heat, but just as he got to you, you fainted so he carried you in here out of the sun. We want you to rest now until your head clears. Chet thinks you may need a little nourishment, so I've ordered a light lunch for you. It'll be here shortly."

Jessica thought Emily and the doctor looked like they might be slightly older than the handsome one, but she really wasn't good at judging people's ages. In fact, the two men had left the room leaving Emily to see to any other details. The lunch came shortly and the waiter followed Emily's gesture to bring it to the coffee table. "Eat very slowly and drink plenty of the liquid," Emily instructed. "I ordered two large lemonades which you'll most likely need to help hydrate your system."

"Emily, I'm so sorry to have been a problem, but could you please tell me where I am? I know I was walking on the beach this morning, but I'm not sure how far I went."

"You got to the Beachside Resort which is

toward the south of Big Breaker Beach, and you'd been walking for quite a while from the looks of your fragile condition. Do you remember when you started out this morning and from where?" It got terribly hot quite quickly today so it wouldn't have taken long for you to be affected by that sun."

"I left my bag at the bus station early this morning, probably about 7:00 or so, and then walked to the beach and just kept going. I wasn't even sure which direction I was heading until I happened to see that the sun was on my left. I just knew I had to get away."

"My goodness, Jessica, you must've been walking for hours and in this horrible heat for at least the last two or three. No wonder you passed out. Did you have food or at least some water with you?"

"I don't think so. I do remember sitting down on the sand and trying to make a sand castle, but I was never very good at that. When my family went to the beach, my sisters used to always laugh at my lopsided attempts."

"My castles always turned out like the leaning tower of Pisa," Emily replied and then had to giggle as she remembered the vacations when C.J. and T.J. would tease her relentlessly about her building technique in the sand. "Right now, however, you need to eat your lunch and then try to get some rest. I have to get back to my desk, but if you should need anything, just ring this and I'll come running." Grinning, she set a small bell on the table by the couch.

Jessica was alone, but she actually felt at peace. She didn't understand why things had happened as they had, but she knew God had rescued her from a life of possible abuse.

Thank you, Dear Jesus, for my timely rescue. The three involved with all this care seem to be such wonderful people, and I only hope I can finish the last few weeks of school and get my diploma without a confrontation with Todd.

She enjoyed the lunch of cottage cheese, a selection of fruits, and a slice of fresh banana nut bread. She was quite surprised when she'd almost finished the two large glasses of lemonade. She lay back on the couch and in minutes was asleep.

CHAPTER TWO

When Jessica awoke, the lights in the room had been turned on, and she could see that it was almost dark outside. She let out a moan as she realized she'd missed the bus she'd planned to take back to school. Her head was hurting now and her skin felt tight and warm, which meant she would probably end up with a bad burn. She was glancing around for a bathroom when her tall handsome rescuer came in from the outer office.

"Well, Jessica, do you feel a little rested now? I see the sun did a very good job of giving you a nice red skin to start your summer tan. You can find some lotion in the bath room right off the kitchen over there that you should apply as you freshen up. Emily and I thought you might like to join us for dinner. She stayed later than usual, in case she was needed, so I owe her a meal. We'd like to have you eat with us."

"You have all been so nice, but I don't want to intrude on your meal together."

He chuckled, "It's no big deal. Whenever Emily can put in a few minutes overtime, she makes me pay with a meal so she doesn't have to go home and cook. Of course, it also gives me someone to eat with. Please, come join us."

"I do need to freshen up, and I'd love to take you up on your offer of the lotion. My skin really does feel tight and a little warm. I'm sorry my clothes are all in a locker at the bus station. I had planned on going back to campus this evening." She picked up her tote bag and started off to freshen up as best she could, but hesitated and said, "I could really use a Tylenol if there'd be one handy."

"I'll get one for you. Come on out to the lobby when you're ready. No hurry."

When they were seated at a table in the resort restaurant, C.J. was the first to speak,

"You mentioned that you were planning to go back to campus this evening. Your spring break isn't over yet, is it? I thought most were just getting started."

"Mine was cut short for personal reasons I'd rather not talk about. It was foolish of me to come in the first place."

"You also mentioned earlier, when we were waiting for the lunch to come, that you just knew you had to get away. Are you in some kind of trouble, Jessica?" Emily asked.

"Oh, yes, probably one of those love at first sight things," C.J. interjected. "I can see it so plainly now. Girl comes to beach, either with a boy or quickly meets boy and the love scene begins--but then there's a quarrel in the love nest and the girl runs off hoping he'll come find her and, of course, promise to love her forever more. Is that about right?" he remarked rather smugly and disgustedly.

"No, Sir, not really," she frowned as she tried to understand why he'd thought of her as that kind of one night stand girl. "Todd and I had been dating for about sixteen months, and he had taken me home to meet his parents and to visit several times. He then begged me to come here with him over spring break, and he even reserved a big two-bedroom suite because I believe in abstaining from sex before marriage. After we'd eaten, we went to our suite and sat on the balcony for awhile, but then he told me he'd changed his mind. During the argument, he also informed me that he'd been getting his satisfaction elsewhere on the campus but intended to have me while we were at the beach. That is why I left. I locked myself in my room, and when I was sure he was asleep, I walked to the bus station and was hoping to return to school before he knew I was gone."

"I'm sorry, Jessica. I should never have prejudged. That was rude of me, but in this business you see so many odd things going on that you can grow indifferent and sometimes misjudge those who are really trying to do the right thing. I'm truly sorry for my remarks."

"C.J. and I both have a deep Christian faith," Emily chimed in. "We've thought that was why we work so well together. It's wonderful to see a young college girl defending her faith because it's rather rare these days, especially here at the beach on spring break."

As they finished their meal, they learned a little more about the situation and then it was decided that Emily would take Jessica home with her for the night, picking up her bag at the bus station on the way. Before they left, C.J. asked if she would please come and talk with him again tomorrow before she made any decisions.

Jessica was afraid she would have a nightmare about Todd, but she felt as if she was in a fantasy world, and it continued throughout the night. She dreamed about being in C.J.'s arms again and he was carrying her into a beautiful castle. He was so attentive and those gorgeous brown eyes looked as if he was truly captivated by her. *Why am I dreaming these things? I hardly know the man and my mind has never gone so awry like this before.* She'd awakened and started to turn over in one of the twin beds in Emily's bedroom, and she quietly mumbled, "Pull yourself together, Jessica."

"Did you say something, Jessica?" Emily asked. "I didn't mean to wake you, but I thought maybe you needed something and didn't know where to find it."

"No, Emily, I'm sorry if I woke you. I was having a rather bizarre dream and told myself to get it together. Now that we're both awake, though, I'd love to get a drink of water and visit the bathroom. Must be all that lemonade you had me drink," she giggled and then asked, "Would you possibly have another Tylenol I could take?"

"Right on. I'll get one and a glass of cold water while you're in the bathroom. Do you remember how to find it? Go down the hallway and it's the first door on your left."

"Thanks, Emily, I'm so sorry I disturbed you. What time is it anyway?"

"It's a little before 4 o'clock. We can get another couple hours of sleep before our day begins. I try to get to the Beachside a little before 8 o'clock each morning so I can relieve the night shift, so I usually get up around 6:00."

Back at the resort, C.J. lay awake for hours trying to sort out the strange thoughts and feelings he was having about this Jessica. *She'd seemed so honest about her problem, but was her story on the level or is she a real shrewd one trying to work her way into my life? There have been way too many cunning schemes over the last five years, since I've been here at Beachside, so I've become leery of most females between 19 and 30. I'd love to find a real*

soul-mate again and have a couple of kids, but how can you trust anyone?

He uttered a prayer, "God, my guide and my comforter, I pray that someday you'll bring the right person into my life. I know I've talked to you before about this, but I'd love to have a wife and family, and I remember my heart beating overtime when I first lifted this Jessica into my arms. Could she be the one you've brought to me? I'm so suspicious of all young women anymore, so please help me, Lord, to be less judgmental and look for the good in Jessica who could possibly be the answer to my prayers."

He finally fell asleep and was surprised that his dreams were all about Jessica. He was holding her in his arms, they were dancing cheek to cheek, and just as he was about to kiss her, he woke up. Looking toward the sky, he asked, "Are you going to let me get a real kiss then, Jesus, or are you going to make me continue to suffer and just remain a real lonely and unhappy guy? This girl has gotten to me, much more than any I've met since I lost Peggy, so I definitely need your guidance.

You know she's a Christian, she's truly a beautiful blonde with the most expressive blue eyes, about 5'4" tall which is a good height to protect, and what a figure! Oops, I'm sorry, Lord," he chuckled, "but it appears she may need some comforting after a traumatic experience she had with her boyfriend. Am I the one you've picked to give it to her? I don't know how good I am at counseling, but I'm ready and willing to try if you brought her here for that reason. Just give me the sign and Em and I will try our best to help her."

A little before 8 o'clock, he was watching from the one-way window in his office as Emily and Jessica arrived. They both appeared to be happy and rested, which was more than he could say for himself. He was amused as he saw his night clerk checking Jessica out with an admiring glance and then, as Emily apparently said something to him, he took off rather quickly. "I wonder if I can get Em to tell me what that had been about? Probably not," he chuckled.

He was checking the mail, a few minutes later, when a knock on the door reminded him that he had asked Jessica to come by to see him before she made any decisions about leaving. For some reason, he didn't want her to just walk out of his life. He certainly didn't understand these odd feelings he was having, so he needed some time to check them out. He wasn't even sure what he was going to say to her, but he had asked for God's guidance earlier and he quickly prayed again, "Father, please don't let me down here."

When he opened the door, Emily was there with Jessica. "You asked her to come see you before she made any decisions, so here she is." Just then the phone started ringing and she said, "I've gotta go," and she hurried off to the front desk.

Smiling, C.J. motioned for Jessica to come in. His

office was as spacious as his apartment had been, and she was totally impressed. A big, highly polished cherry desk was accented with an outstanding desk lamp, a gold trimmed name plate, and other gold desk items and accessories. Behind his leather chair were bookcases and file cabinets also in cherry. He held a chair for her to sit in that was upholstered in a rich burgundy fabric with a large sailboat embroidered on the back. She smiled as she wondered if he really had a sailboat to relax in whenever he got a chance.

"Well, Jessica, you appear to have recovered from your ordeal yesterday, and I'm glad we could be there for you. I think the lotion must have helped because your face isn't as red as it was last night. But, let's talk a little about your plans, now that it appears you don't have a place to stay and you were going to take a bus back to school without even getting to enjoy a full day of your spring break. Is that what you really want to do or would you like to stay here on the beach for a few days? I have an option for you, since you mentioned last night that you liked to work with small kids and wanted to teach pre-school." *(How had I ever thought of this plan when* my *mind had been a complete blank?)*

He then continued, "We provide a sitting service for the families who are staying at the Beachside so the moms and dads can enjoy a few hours by themselves while they're on vacation. It has proven to be very much appreciated, but it just happens that our babysitter is going to a big family wedding in

Chicago and will be gone from Wednesday through Sunday next week. We don't offer this service on Sundays, so I was wondering if you would consider taking her place for those four days? That would give you Monday and Tuesday to spend with Jackie, getting a little familiar with the routine, and still enjoy some time on the beach. When there are no calls for sitters, you'd also have free time. The pay isn't too bad, really, and we'll make sure that you get back to school by Sunday night. It would be a great help to us because, otherwise, we'll have to close the service while Jackie is gone."

Jessica was stunned. How could such amazing things be happening to her when she had felt her world crumbling around her 24 hours ago? She looked at him to make sure he was real before she opened her mouth to speak. "I really don't know what to say, C.J. It sounds too good to be true, and you know the saying about that, don't you?" she giggled.

"But if you're really serious, I would love to stay and help out. Just one problem, though, I only have the clothes I brought for the beach."

"You'll still be on the beach, so any clothes you brought should be appropriate for sitting with the little ones. I really doubt it, but Jackie may be about your size, so we'll check with her and see if she may have some extras if you think you'll need them. No way could you wear Emily's clothes, with her tall tomboyish frame, but she'll probably insist you stay with her again tonight because she loves having company."

"I don't think Emily is tall or tomboyish, but are you sure she'd want to have me intruding? I've slept on the floor many times growing up with two sisters and having all the overnighters, so I would be willing to curl up on the playroom floor for those few nights."

She had noticed that C.J. had the cutest smile, which he again exhibited as he assured her that she'd not be sleeping on the floor of the playroom. "There's a small room off the playroom that has a lavatory, shower and stool, so if we don't have a vacancy, we'll put a bed in there and you'll be able to use it until there is a regular room available. We'll put a screen up that will give the bed privacy if the little ones need to use the facilities. As I've mentioned, the service is not open on Sundays so you can enjoy today doing whatever you want. There's a church about two blocks from here, and if you'd like to go with Emily and me, we'll be leaving about 10:15 for the 10:30 service. The dress code is beach wear, excluding swim suits, of course, so you're fine in what you have on. Our cashier attends early mass on Sundays and then watches the desk so Emily, the real tomboy, can attend church services at 10:30." He grinned but then couldn't keep from laughing when she gave him a disapproving look.

"That's not nice, C.J.," she smiled, "but thank you. I'd love to go to church services with you and the very pretty Emily." She stood to leave, and he hurried around to open the door for her.

"You can check with the tomboy about anything you'd like to know about the resort and the area, and I'll see you just a little later. Thanks again, Jessica, I feel God has truly answered a prayer." He couldn't keep from chuckling as he closed the door. He sank into his chair, put his elbows on the desk and placed his chin in his hands. "God, you are amazing," he prayed, "because I would never have thought to ask her to take Jackie's place this week. I'm wondering, however, are you doing this for her or for me? I guess, which ever, she'll be around for a few days and maybe I can get all these feelings I've been having under control before she walks out of my life."

Jessica went to the desk to tell Emily that she would be staying the whole week to fill in for Jackie, but she couldn't keep from looking a little closer at the wonderful friend she had made yesterday and who C.J. had referred to as the 'real tomboy'. She was about 5'7" she would guess, truly a brunette with brown eyes and a beautiful olive skin. She may be a little larger boned, but definitely not over-weight or tomboyish. As far as Jessica was concerned, Emily was a beautiful girl, and one who was thrilled with the news about her staying for the week.

She then roamed around the halls, went outside and looked around the pool, and got a drink from the vending machine. She got back to the desk at 10:15 and found Emily busy with a check-out, but C.J. was just coming from his office. They were soon on their way to the Sunday worship service.

Jessica thought the whole service had been very interesting. Emily had managed, somehow, to have C.J. sit between the two of them, but he didn't seem to mind. She just supposed, if he and Emily came together every week, he was used to sitting with her so what was one more. She'd loved the hymns that had been selected as they were based on the promises God has given us and the thanks we should give in return. The sermon was about the importance of prayer and relying on all those promises God had made and what He does for us each day. We need to keep in touch with Him in our daily prayers. She was definitely ready to thank Him when there was time for a silent prayer before the pastor prayed aloud.

After the service, C.J. and Emily were both approached and greeted by several as they were leaving, so she felt that they were known in a good way around the area.

CHAPTER THREE

When they returned to the Beachside, they went to the very nice deli in the resort that handles the lunch crowd. Emily quickly ordered a sandwich and drink to go because she needed to get back to the desk, but C.J. asked Jessica if she would join him. When she agreed, he then led her to a booth. "What can I get you, or would you like to place your own order?" he asked with a smile. "I'll be happy to be your personal server."

She could feel her heart start thumping in her chest, something she had never felt with Todd, but she quickly brought her thoughts back to answer his question. "I'd like to have a chicken salad sandwich and a small lemonade, if you'd like to be my personal server," she giggled. She hoped she could calm down while he was away.

Bowing slightly, he grinned as he went to the counter to place their orders.

As she glanced around, she saw that it was a very clean deli, and the aromas of the food coming from the kitchen were really tantalizing. The decor was a nice soft taupe on the walls with a large border of sailboats around the top. Several great pictures of boats and barges decorated the spaces between the windows. The tabletops were also taupe, but the booths had burgundy leather on the seats and a nice soft padded fabric on the backs.

"It's just a little early," he said as he placed the tray of food on the table and slid in across from her, "but I usually eat when we return from church. If all is well around here, then I sneak out for awhile on my sailboat. I was wondering if you would consider joining me, Jessica, but maybe you don't like boating."

After seeing the sailboats on the chairs in his office, Jessica had to smile when she realized that his love for sailing must have carried over to his office furniture. She was still recalling the unbelievable things that had happened to her since being rescued yesterday when she heard C.J. softly calling her name. She was so embarrassed and knew her cheeks had to be turning a bright red as she remembered he'd asked her a question. She thought it best to be truthful, so she said, "I'm sorry, C.J., but I was thinking about all the things that have happened to me in the last 24 hours, especially when you mentioned your sailboat. It caused me to remember seeing the sailboats embroidered on your office chairs and I had wondered then if you had a sailboat to get away on. So you really do have one? I've never been on a sailboat, but I have been on some runabouts and fishing boats, so I'm sure your sailboat would be fun, too. I've always loved watching them from the shore. They appear to be so graceful as they move along."

There was that cute smile again as he said, "So, are you stalling for some reason or did you forget my question?"

"I guess I was stalling a little. It's hard for me to put my Friday night experience out of my mind, and I had known Todd for a year and a half. Then I realize I've only known you for 24 hours so I'm wondering just how vulnerable I would be out on the water in a sailboat. As much as I'd love to go sailing, I'm sort of scared, too. Can you understand how my feelings may be a little confusing?"

"Yes, I certainly can, Jessica, and I respect you for it. Since I bought the Beachside five years ago, I've felt as though I was being pursued constantly by women just begging to go on the boat, wanting to take me to dinner or maybe directly to their room. It might surprise you to learn that I have never had a woman on my boat. I really don't know why I asked you today except that I felt I'd like to get to know you better. It just seemed like a nice, quiet place so we could talk. It sounds rather silly coming from a man, I suppose, but I feel quite comfortable with you after such a short time," he chuckled.

"Thank you, C.J., I appreciate that and I've been very comfortable with you, too. It felt as though we were supposed to be friends right from the start, except for your first accusation, of course," she smiled rather accusingly. She took a bite of her sandwich and then watched as he did the same. "If you're going sailing, wouldn't you usually take your lunch with you and eat it on the boat? That really sounds like fun on a beautiful day like today."

"Are you considering coming with me, then? We'll eat our sandwiches and drink our drinks and then I'll show you how to make the sails and the wind take you where you want to go. And, Jessica, I promise, as God is my witness, that I will not touch you inappropriately. So, will you please come with me?"

"You are very convincing, C.J., but we'd better go before I change my mind. You just remember, you have a reputation to protect here and I expect you to keep your promise to me and to God. I can swim pretty well, but I'd prefer not having to from way out there."

"I promise, I really do, that you'll be safe with me."

They stopped at his apartment long enough for him to get a small cooler that would hold their sandwiches and drinks, some ice, some grapes and some bottles of water, and to also let Emily know where they would be.

"Do you have your cell phone?" Emily asked. He nodded as he took Jessica's hand and headed toward the marina about a block away. As they walked along, he just couldn't believe the tingles going up his arm and down his spine as he continued holding her hand. It just felt so right.

Emily stood watching and grinning as she'd noticed the difference in C.J. since he'd held Jessica in his arms yesterday when he'd carried her in from the beach. *He'd acted as though she'd become a part of him the moment he'd touched her, as if God had guided him to her for a purpose. And Jessica, the sweet and the innocent, but also so very strong in her faith, needs a man like C.J. to love, cherish and protect her. So what if they're only going for a boat ride this afternoon. I can dream, can't I?*

Jessica was surprised at how quiet the motor ran as they started out of the marina. Of course, she realized they were moving at 'no wake' speed, but compared to the runabouts she had ridden on, it was very quiet. When they reached the open water, he adjusted the sails and cut the motor. They sat side by side as they were eating their sandwiches and enjoying their cold drinks, and their conversation went easily. They talked about their families, her two older sisters, his one older brother, their youth and schooling, how he had been able to buy the resort, and their dreams for the future.

She was really amazed at the number of boats that were out this afternoon, and she was mesmerized by the soft waves as she watched them forming patterns on the water. The scenery along the shore suddenly drew her attention and she felt herself staring to see if they would possibly go by the hotel where she and Todd had been staying. "Are we going north so we'll sail pass all the resorts on Breaker Beach?" she asked as she wondered if they could be recognized by the people on the sand or in the water.

"No, Jessica, we're not going north." Realizing her apprehension about being seen by Todd, he continued. "Although I'd doubt that anyone could recognize us at this distance, I decided to sail south to eliminate any chance."

"Thanks, C.J., I'm sorry to be such a problem to you, but I can't seem to forget that I may still be in harm's way if Todd were to find me."

"We'll handle that, Jessica, if it arises, but for now please just relax and enjoy the nice sunshiny afternoon and restful ride."

After they'd finished eating, he was soon ready to give her a lesson in sailing, but it didn't take long for him to realize she knew a lot about boats, just not about sails. She was a quick learner as he explained how the sails are raised and what you have to do to change directions, and she was soon doing it perfectly, but when he'd put his arms around her to show her the way to work some of the other lines, he felt a definite reluctance to cooperate.

"Jessica, I'm sorry if this disturbs you, but I need to be at this position to show you the right way to hold the line. Would you rather I not do anymore teaching today?"

"I...think that...would be...best," she stammered as she ducked out from under his arm and sat down on the seat across the stern. "I...also think...I'm ready... to go in."

He glanced at his watch and was shocked to realize that they had been out for almost three hours. Rarely did he stay out over an hour and a half when he was alone. "Yes, I see that it is definitely time to head in. The time sort of got away from me. I usually don't stay out this long, so I guess good company certainly does makes a difference," he grinned.. "It will probably take another 30 minutes to reach the marina so would you like to go inside on the way back? Are you getting a little too much sun or need the facilities?"

"Yes, that would be nice. Do you stay up here to get us in safely?"

Realizing she was still upset and needed to be away from him, he said, "Yes, I'll need to be up here at the docking. Will you be all right by yourself?"

"I'll come back out if I don't like it inside by myself," she giggled.

The giggle made him feel a little better as he opened the hatch door for her and she slipped inside. Luckily he'd been heading for the marina so it wasn't long until he could lower the sails and start the engine. While he was doing that, he was also saying a prayer that he hoped he hadn't made her afraid of him this afternoon. His feelings toward her had only increased and he would be devastated if she turned away from him now. He knew he wanted to get to know her better and he also felt that God had something to do with all of what was happening.

Emily had been so glad that C.J. had convinced Jessica to go with him this afternoon because a young man had come to the resort inquiring about a college student with blonde hair, blue eyes, 5'4" tall and very pretty. He'd said he was worried about her as she had wandered away from their hotel yesterday and he hadn't been able to find her. He'd been told that she may have been seen around this resort.

Emily had asked him if he had gone to the authorities, and he'd said he didn't want to do that. He just wanted to find her because she had been upset when she'd left.

"Do you know why she was upset?" she'd asked, but then he'd gotten hostile.

"That's none of your business!" he'd almost shouted, "because it's just between me and her, so if you know anything about where she might be, you'd better tell me. There are a few things I need to get her straightened out about, and she'd better listen. But they are just our problems, and they certainly don't concern you or anyone else."

Emily had noticed that he'd sounded quite sure of

himself, but she still calmly replied, "Well, I'm sorry you feel that way because your problems might be between you, her, and her God."

He'd then turned and walked away, mumbling, "Just another one of those over religious people, so why should I even waste my time?" *Because I know why I need to find her, and I won't give up because I want her while she's still a virgin. With all these college guys here on the beach, she could be quite a target.*

CHAPTER FOUR

When Jessica and C.J. got back to the resort, it was almost 4:15 and Emily was off duty. However, she was waiting and immediately approached them. "I need to talk to you, C.J. Something happened while you were gone that I think you should know about."

Assuming it was business, he asked, "Jessica, would you excuse us for just a few minutes so I can tend to this problem?" as he headed for his office. "Is there a problem with one of the rooms, Em?"

She was shaking her head as she said, "No, C.J., it isn't anything concerning the hotel, but I'm afraid Jessica may have a small problem. A young man came in here this afternoon and asked about a pretty blonde with blue eyes and about 5'4". He said she had wandered away from their hotel and she had been upset when she left. I assumed that it was Todd and tried to get some more information from him by asking if he knew why she was upset.

He said the problem was between him and her, but when I mentioned that it could be between him, her, and God, he became rather hostile and stormed out referring to me as another religious person and why should he waste his time. He said someone had told him that she might be here so I don't know if he'll be back or not."

C.J. went to the door and motioned for Jessica to join them. "She's got to know," he said as they waited for her to enter. Emily reiterated the event and Jessica slumped into a chair visibly distraught. "I'd better get my things and catch the bus back to school before I cause you any more trouble. I have no idea what he may try now if he discovers I am really here. I hadn't thought he would even try to find me after our argument Friday night, but could one of you possibly take me to the bus station?"

"You're not going to any bus station," C.J. declared decisively. "You're as entitled to a spring break as he is, and you're going to be doing something to help others while he is playing around on the beach and probably harassing most of the girls. So, let's continue with our original plans and see what happens. I'll keep a close watch on the resort and if you see him, I want you to come to the office immediately. You aren't on duty with the children until Wednesday, so I imagine things will settle down by then."

Turning to Emily, he asked, "Were you planning to take her home with you again tonight, or should I make other arrangements?"

"Of course I'm taking her home with me and I have protection, as you know, if I need it. Do you think we should stay here, though, until it gets dark?"

"I think he would definitely be on the beach at this time of day," Jessica said, "so I'd suggest we leave now unless you want to eat before we go. I don't think he'll leave the beach before 6 or 7 o'clock and probably even later."

"Let's plan to eat before you leave," C.J. eagerly suggested, and Emily barely held back a chuckle. It was now so obvious to her that he didn't want Jessica out of his sight, and it was so endearing. She wondered what had happened on the boat this afternoon because she hadn't seen him this intrigued even with Peggy.

"Would you like to sit on the beach for awhile, Jessica, or is there something else you would like to do?"

"I think she's had plenty of sun for one day, being on the boat," C.J. volunteered very quickly. "Why don't the two of you go into my apartment and relax? Jessica might even be ready for a little nap. There are cold drinks and some snacks, if you're interested. I have a few things to take care of here and then I'll join you."

"He makes a suggestion sound as if it's compulsory, doesn't he?" Jessica chuckled as she and Emily left C.J. to his tasks and entered his apartment. As much as she would love to look around his place, Jessica knew she didn't dare be so bold. She did, however, get to see his kitchen as they rummaged through the refrigerator and pantry to find the snacks he had mentioned. It was well organized, clean, and well-stocked. *I wonder if he has a housekeeper to take care of all the details,* but then she realized where she was and almost laughed aloud. *Of course, this is a resort and cleaning is done every day, so why shouldn't it be spotless.*

She was glancing at the pictures on the walls of the living room and she wanted to investigate more closely the one picture, in particular, hanging over the fireplace. She was sure she recognized it as a famous painting she had seen on special display for a limited time at an art gallery when her family had taken a European tour, but, at the moment, she couldn't remember the artist. *Is it a copy or could it possibly be an original?* She continued to study it as she and Emily had settled down on the sofa.

Emily had turned on the TV and started watching reruns of some of the great old favorites, but Jessica kept thinking about the picture and C.J. *Surely he couldn't afford an original of that quality, could he? Who is this guy, anyway, and who are his parents? He told me, during the conversation about our families, that his folks had helped him with the down payment on the resort, but he hadn't elaborated.*

Her curiosity was growing by the minute, but she turned her attention back to the TV where Emily was now watching a Golden Girls rerun. She had always loved that show and was soon laughing along with Emily because they are so funny, and for the time being, she completely forgot about the picture.

It was about an hour before C.J. entered the apartment, got himself a drink from the fridge and joined them. Jessica was amazed when, without hesitation, he seated himself between them on the couch, gave them that cute grin, and helped himself to the food Emily had found. First he had some crackers and cheese, and then he took a small bunch of grapes, tossed one at a time into the air and expertly caught them in his mouth. He turned to Jessica and fed her one of the grapes, touching his fingers to her lips as he did so. She was so surprised, she felt her cheeks heating up, but before she could do or say a word, he was there with another grape, and tingles were running up and down her arms.

Emily had been so engrossed in the TV show that Jessica hoped she'd missed C.J.'s grape feeding, but Emily hadn't missed a thing and had the most satisfying smile on her face.

It didn't take long for C.J. to devour the plate of snacks as he continued to feed a few grapes to Jessica and ate several more himself. "Hey, Em, isn't there something better on that TV than all those old reruns? How about a basketball game?" He reached for the remote, but she held it away from him while shaking her head.

"Not until this program is over. You want to watch this, don't you, Jessica?"

"I'm not getting into that argument," she chuckled.

"One way, I don't have a place to sleep tonight, and the other, I'm fired and won't be able to stay here and take care of the little ones, so you two fight it out."

"Poor sport," Emily laughed as the program ended and she handed the remote over to C.J. "What game do you think is on at this time of day, anyway?"

"I don't know. I just wanted to get the remote away from you." As he tried to dodge Emily's swing at him, he lost his balance and fell sideways toward Jessica, actually landing across her lap. They were all laughing so hard that he decided to just lie there for a few seconds and enjoy the softness of her body. "I'm sorry," he said as he tried to push himself up from her lap, but he kept accidentally touching her instead of the couch, and he was afraid she might be panicking.

She finally pushed on his back and helped him sit up so he could look at her face. She didn't appear to be too upset so he turned on Emily and punched her lightly on the arm. "You should be ashamed of yourself, Em." Laughing, he stood up and asked, "Are you girls about ready to go eat? I'm starved after the afternoon on the boat, an early lunch, that tiny snack of grapes and then our little skirmish," he chuckled.

"Just admit that you have a bottomless pit as a stomach, Mr. Peterson, but I guess we'll agree to accompany you to the restaurant to get it filled up. Since you ate most of the snacks, we'll expect you to pick up the tab for dinner, too," Emily teased.

"As if that's something out of the ordinary," he

smirked as he held out his hands to help both of them up off the couch. He gave Emily a little mischievous shove toward the door, and with one of them on each arm, he escorted them to the most enchanting candle-light restaurant. They were seated by the hostess, and it wasn't long before the server had brought the menus, glasses of water, and lit the candle on their table.

The special for the day was grilled salmon, which Jessica loved, so her choice of an entree was very easy. She waited for the other two to make up their minds, and when the server came to take their order, Emily had decided to have the salmon, also. C.J. had, of course, ordered the large T-bone steak. Jessica wondered where he put all that food, but he is definitely over 6' and she had to assume that it took a lot of food to keep him filled up. She couldn't, however, resist asking, "You live here on the beach, C.J., with all the fresh seafood, and you order steak?"

"That is exactly why I ordered steak tonight. I do live here on the beach almost 365 days a year, and I eat all kinds of fish, shrimp, lobster, oysters, clams, crabmeat, tuna, grouper, salmon, you name it, I eat it. There comes a time when a man wants beef," he chuckled.

Their conversation covered a multitude of subjects, from their sailboat ride to what the weather was supposed to be tomorrow. One topic Jessica had brought up was about the decor and furnishings of the restaurants, lobby, his apartment, etc. She realized she'd been too upset last night to notice much about this restaurant, but tonight she was really impressed with the comfort and the relaxing colors in all the areas she had seen. The deep burgundy, which was in his office, was carried throughout the lobby and the more formal restaurant. The lobby is lighted with big, beautiful chandeliers, but the restaurant seemed so cool and relaxing because it is quite subdued with just wall sconces giving off a rather soft glow. There were unlit candles on each table, but the ones on the occupied tables or booths were burning for a rather romantic setting.

"I guess it's a little early for the candles on all the tables to be lit, or is that a special part of the welcome?" she asked.

Emily answered with a chuckle, "They do light the candles as the tables or booths are occupied so all of the candles don't get lit until 9 o'clock or later during the summer months. That's when the tourists decide to leave the beach and realize they're starved.

Both C.J. and Emily had contributed to the story about how badly the place had needed a face-lift, and Emily proudly announced that every decision had personally been made by C.J. "Luckily," she continued, "the former owner had redecorated about half of the rooms and installed new furniture and bathroom fixtures just before the sale. That gave us nice clean rooms to use while the rest were being decorated to C.J.'s specifications. There are just a few left that he wants to remodel, and he's anxious to get them all finished as soon as possible."

"Well, hopefully, with the place staying full like it has this year, we just might be able to get started on some of those during the slow months. Of course, as often as I have to buy you dinner, Em, it may take a bit longer," he laughed.

When they'd finished their main entree, C.J. insisted they have some dessert, so Jessica had strawberry cheesecake, Emily had Dutch apple pie, and C.J. settled for a huge brownie sundae. "They make that special just for him," Emily whispered. Jessica thought they were finished after dessert, but C.J. decided they all needed a cup of coffee so Emily wouldn't fall asleep driving home.

Emily smiled and was ready to agree to any of his suggestions tonight because she understood how he hated to see them leave. She knew C.J. so well because they had not only worked together for five years, but they had grown up as next door neighbors, and his older brother, T.J., had been her first teenage love. He was a year older and, without even knowing, he had broken her young vulnerable heart when he'd paid no attention to her. To him, she was just the little tomboy who lived next door and always tagged along on all the family outings. Of course, her parents had been there, too, because the two families took vacations, went camping, fishing, biking, and hiking every year together as well as a lot of other things, especially the two mothers.

Being two years older than C.J., she'd watched him go from puppy love, to real love, to heartbreak, to indifference. Her hopes and prayers now are for this to be a new beginning for her sweet, wonderful friend and boss. Jessica seems to be just the type of personality to match C.J.'s love of fun and sun that she'd grown to know, and his actions yesterday and today have convinced her that he has noticed the difference between Jessica and those other girls who have tried to get his attention. Maybe it was the fact that Jessica needed him when she appeared struggling on the beach yesterday, but whatever it was, C.J. is now definitely interested in a girl who would fit in his world.

CHAPTER FIVE

C.J. walked them to Emily's car to make sure Todd wouldn't be waiting to cause some kind of trouble. He watched as they backed out of the parking space and headed south and then west toward Emily's condo. He'd never thought to ask Jessica which hotel Todd would be staying at, but since the Beachside Resort is almost the last one before you leave Breaker Beach, he didn't feel apprehensive that they would possibly meet him tonight. However, he decided he would call in about twenty minutes to make sure they got to Em's safe and sound.

On the way home to Emily's, Jessica thought again about the picture hanging over the fireplace, so she decided to ask. "The picture over C.J.'s fireplace looks so much like a famous painting that was part of an estate on loan in a European art gallery over ten years ago, but I can't remember the artist's name.

I was thinking it was Rembrandt, but do you know if it is or not?"

"You're right," Emily answered with a chuckle. "It is a Rembrandt and, of course, there's a story behind it. His mother's parents and grandparents, and possibly even the great grandparents, own an exquisite Antique store, but they specialize in handling expensive art pieces from estates, etc. His mother, Jeanette, had worked there while she attended college and even after she was married to his dad, who was finishing his residency. She enjoyed it so much, she decided to continue helping her parents, after the grandparents retired, and then took it over when her parents decided they wanted to do some traveling.

Their two boys were teenagers by then, and C.J. had expressed a love of sailboats and sailing since he was about ten. When this painting came in, as part of an estate, Jeanette immediately called his dad, Brian, and asked his opinion. Of course, he rushed over to see it, they quickly agreed it had to be C.J.'s when he had a place to put it, and they made a deal with the executor of the estate. They had it hanging over the fireplace in their den for several years, but when C.J. bought the Beachside Resort and had the apartment almost gutted and redecorated, the painting became his. You can't imagine the look on his face when Brian and Jeannette arrived with the painting in their car. He told me that he used to sit in their den for hours just looking at that painting and dreaming that he was in a boat of his own out on the ocean. Of course, he'd never dreamed of being caught in a storm like in the picture."

"Wow, that's quite a story," Jessica remarked as Emily turned into her driveway and on into the garage. The phone started ringing shortly after they'd entered the kitchen, and Emily grinned as she answered, and Jessica listened to one side of the conversation.

"Yes, C.J., we got home safely.... . ..Yes, the doors are locked, the car is in the garage, and I think we're heading to bed shortly... . .We are so stuffed from all that food you made us eat, we can't do much else but sleep it off. . . You get some sleep, too. . . We'll see you in the morning. . . Goodnight, C.J."

They did decide to watch the late news on TV, but as they both started yawning, they grinned and headed for the bedroom. "I'm really sorry I haven't furnished the other room as a bedroom, but I use it for my computer room, my sewing room, and my exercise room. In fact, I'd better check my e-mail so you go ahead and get ready for bed."

"The twin beds are great so don't be sorry. But Emily, I've heard C.J. call you Em a few times since I've been around. Would you mind if I called you that, too?"

"I'd love for you to call me Em. Has anyone given you a nickname for Jessica?"

"My two sisters call me Jess once in a while, but my parents don't appreciate it very much. If you want to call me that, though, I wouldn't mind at all. The kids at school never seemed to pick up on a nickname."

"I doubt if it'll be too long before C.J. does. He loves to shorten everybody's name. I bet the kids were afraid to call you Jess, thinking you'd resent being called a name which is more commonly used for boys. If they'd heard your parents or sisters call you Jess, they most likely would've done it, too. I sort of like Jessie and may use that. But head for bed now, I'll be right with you."

Jessica picked up her bag and headed for the bedroom and some shuteye. As she got into her gown, she relived the day she had thoroughly enjoyed, but why had Todd spoiled it by trying to find her? She realized how much she dreaded going back to college and having to face him. "I wish I knew if I had enough credits to graduate without going to classes the last few remaining weeks. I'd love to stay and find another job around here after this week is over." She was still mumbling to herself as Emily came into the room.

"Talking to yourself, Jessie?" Emily asked and giggled. "I thought I heard you saying something about finding a job around here after this week is over. Did I happen to hear you correctly?"

"Oh, I was just daydreaming, Em, but I did enjoy myself so much today. I always did love the beach, and I was wondering if I might possibly have enough credits that I would be able to graduate without finishing the year. I just dread going back and having to face Todd."

"I probably shouldn't tell you this, but I think it could help you to understand C.J. a little better if you knew some of his history. I know him quite well because we grew up as neighbors, and I've been working for him at the Resort now for over five years.

He had a rough time in college because his girlfriend died of meningitis. They had both been juniors. They'd started dating in high school and had planned to be married soon after they'd finished college. When she was hospitalized, he went to be with her, but she was under quarantine and he could only watch her through a window. He wouldn't move and he stood and watched as she took her last breath. He hasn't been able to forgive himself or even start to forget. He felt it had to be his fault, that he must've done something wrong to cause God to take her away from him. He became indifferent toward life, and his family was very concerned that he might not want to live until he heard about the Beachside Resort being for sale. He was only 23, or almost 24, but his parents saw an interest in his eyes for the first time in three years. They discussed it with him and were quick to offer the money for the down payment and other start-up expenses when he remarked that he'd love to own a resort on the beach but didn't have that kind of money. They may have just made him a loan, but he has made it a very profitable investment.

I don't think you could even start to imagine

the number of girls who have thrown themselves at him since he's been here. He is always polite, but lets them know that he's not interested. That is, until you showed up. I saw such a difference in him when he was carrying you into the lobby and how he has wanted to care for you and have you near him as much as possible.

I don't know what your feelings are, Jessie, but please don't hurt him, I beg of you. I'm sure it's too soon for you to have any kind of deep feelings, but I'd like to ask you to let him take the initiative and just see where it goes. You are the type of girl he needs, I know your faith has impressed him, and I feel he'd do anything to protect you from Todd or anyone else who would want to hurt you."

"Oh, Em, thank you so much for telling me this. I feel that I understand his actions so much better than I did before. I'm not sure where my feelings are right now, especially after that experience with Todd, but I'll be very careful around C.J."

"Not too careful as to arouse suspicions, or I'll be in trouble big time," she laughed.

"He'd be ready to fire me if he knew I had confided in you. Please, just continue being the girl we've gotten to know, okay?"

Letting out a big yawn, Jessica giggled as she said, "I'll just be myself, but right now it has to be Goodnight, Irene, Goodnight, Ms. Em. I may see you in my dreams."

"So true. Goodnight, Jessie."

What a wonderful night's rest, Jessica thought, when she opened her eyes and saw the sun peeking in the windows. She heard the shower so knew Emily was up and getting ready for work. She was anxious, too, to meet Jackie, see the playroom, and maybe even get to play with some little ones today. She just hoped there'd be some parents who wanted time to spend together without their little ones.

She had just sat up on the edge of the bed when Emily came out of the bathroom in her robe and slippers. "I'm going to get the coffee brewing now so you can shower if you'd like. Did you sleep well after all my ramblings last night?"

"I slept very well as I dreamed about being rocked in the boat and I didn't even get scared this time when C.J. put his arms around me to show me how to work the sails."

"Well, that sounds like a great improvement. See you in a few minutes," Emily let out a chuckle as she headed toward the kitchen which was just down the hall.

Jessica showered quickly and got dressed in a pair of cut-off jeans and a bright hot pink top that she thought the little ones would like. She remembered how they'd liked the bright colors when she was student teaching. She also pulled her long, natural curly hair into a ponytail to prevent a little one from grabbing it and not letting go. She'd learned from experience that the pulling of her hair by a little one could be quite painful. Just then the smell of coffee drifted into the room so she joined Emily in the kitchen for that great wake-up cup of latte.

Not only was there coffee, but Emily had fixed waffles with fresh strawberries and whipped cream for a wonderful breakfast. "What does C.J. do for breakfast?" Jessica asked as she was devouring this wonderful waffle along with a second cup of coffee.

"Oh, don't worry about C.J. He is a good cook, if he wants to cook, but he also has the chef ready to fix whatever he desires anytime of day. The whole staff adores him, Jessie, and it didn't take them long to grasp that something had definitely happened to him when he had you in his arms as well as the sequence of things happening since then. They have all been working for him since he became owner, and I doubt that you'd find even one of them who would think about leaving no matter what another hotel might offer."

"There is certainly something about him that draws a person to him. Even when he made the remark about a love at first sight affair that first night, I couldn't quite take it as a condemnation since it seemed like he was just trying to find out what kind of a person I was."

"I was a little surprised when he made that remark, but after seeing how so many girls had been trying to get his attention, I guess I can understand his hesitation about accepting a girl, no matter how he was feeling about her, without delving a little into her personal life. But, I think it's about time for us to be on our way now. A lot of people are ready to get on their way early in the morning, and they need an extra pair of hands to check them out."

CHAPTER SIX

As Emily and Jessica walked into the lobby a few minutes before eight, Jessica had noticed C.J. standing there with a woman about her size, but at least thirty years older. Her face must have shown her surprise, because both of them started smiling.

The woman looked at C.J. and started laughing. "You didn't tell her that I'm actually a grandmother, did you?" she asked as she punched him in the arm playfully. Coming forward to the two girls, she greeted Emily and then extended her hand to Jessica. "Hi, Jessica, I'm Jackie Olin, whom you expected to be one of those young, energetic babysitters, I imagine. I apologize for C.J.'s obvious neglect to tell you that I just turned fifty-three and my husband, Daryl, and I are both going to Chicago to attend our only daughter's wedding. I work to supplement my husband's disability check from Black Lung Disease plus some other income from a few investments that we have.

I'm so elated they won't have to close the babysitting program while I'm gone, so would you like to come with me now and see the playroom and check some of the things we try to do with the smaller children?"

"I'd love to, Jackie." After waving to C.J. and Emily, they started off toward the play room and Jessica continued, "I'm sorry I looked so surprised, but I had no idea who to expect as neither C.J. nor Emily told me anything about you. You mentioned being a grandmother--to how many?"

We only have one son, James, and one daughter, Eileen, whose wedding we're going to.. James and his wife were married a little over three years ago and have one little boy, James Daryl Olin. He is definitely a hand full at 9 months old. James is 30, and after working with his grandfather, great uncle, and uncle for eight years, he is now managing the Do-It-Yourself Center in Wilmington in the buildings that my parents opened in 1945. Dad had just returned from his Army service in the World War II.

It started out as a small lumberyard, but Dad got his older brother to come in with him and they worked it into a good thriving business. My brother joined them in 1968, just out of college, and he suggested the Do-It-Yourself Center. It really did well over the years, and James is doing a very good job of continuing all the services that the others had started. Dad drops in about once a week to see him and is very impressed.

My parents live in a Retirement Home in Wilmington now, but they are both still quite active. My uncle and aunt are both gone, leaving no heirs, so they willed their part of the business to our son. My brother and his wife moved out west two years ago after they had taken several vacations to Colorado, Utah, Nevada, and California. They decided it was where they definitely wanted to live when they retired. After their older daughter had met and married a career Naval Officer and was living near San Diego, he actually retired rather young, made all of the financial arrangements with our son to buy them out over a period of years, and then moved with the younger daughter, to St. George, Utah. They hadn't really been impressed on their trips to California, but Utah was still close enough to their daughter so they could visit quite often.

James did a lot of remodeling to my parents' home to bring it up to date, and now he and his family live there, so we have kept most everything in the family.

Now, you've heard my whole story except about my husband and me. I met my husband while I was attending college in Virginia. Even though his family had little money, I was so in love with him that I would've lived in a hut, and almost did for awhile. Over the years, working in the mines, he developed the black lung disease. My parents made sure our son and daughter had a good education—they both graduated from UNC.

Finally, we convinced Daryl to take disability, and the family urged us to come down here and live in the vacation home my parents had bought during my early teens. James had some renovations done there, too, so it is a marvelous home for just the two of us. I'd always remembered spending such wonderful times there on the beach, and the family felt the fresh ocean air would be good for Daryl. We persuaded him to at least give it a try. That was ten years ago and there has been a great improvement in his health.

My uncle and aunt, as I mentioned, left their part of the business to James, gave an equal amount in cash to Eileen, and the rest to Daryl and me. With good advice, we were able to invest so we receive a monthly income from the interest it earns. Mom and Dad have also helped a lot along the way. Have I talked your ears off yet?"

Laughing, they realized they had arrived at the playroom sometime ago and Jessica had been impressed with the whole setup as she had been with Jackie herself. What a great family story, and what a great room in which to entertain the little ones.

Just then the door opened and C.J. walked in with two darling little boys. "We found these two little guys wanting someplace to play and have some fun," he smiled. "Their parents expect to be back by lunchtime." Putting his hand on one of the little heads, he said, "This is Darren, and this is Warren," as he changed his hand from one to the other. He told the boys that these two ladies are Jackie and Jessica, and they're looking forward to keeping you happy."

Jackie was immediately down on her knees so she would be at their height. Her smile would melt anyone's heart, and she certainly made a good first impression on these two little ones. She easily led them to some of the toys that would interest their age group, and she showed them how to work a mechanical lift on a big construction rig that one of the boys had picked up but looked perplexed on how it worked. Jessica was again impressed and knew she had to get more familiar with the toys before she was on her own Wednesday.

She looked up and saw C.J. still standing there watching Jackie with the boys but then he turned his eyes to look at her. She noticed how his eyes sparkled and that gorgeous grin, which made her skin tingle, was enough to send her into a tailspin. *Why am I so giddy when I only met this guy two days ago?* She returned his smile as she walked over to him.

"They are really cute, aren't they?" she asked quietly. She felt rather speechless when his eyes seemed to always be searching hers, so this had been just something to say to break the spell they seemed to be under.

"Oh, yes, *little boys* are always cute," he remarked. "It's when they grow up that they can become ugly, demanding, and self-centered. I'm sorry,I didn't mean to say that. I've just been thinking too much, I'm afraid, and that is never good in my case. I'd better get back to the office. Can I take you and Jackie to lunch when the parents get back?"

"If we don't have anymore little ones show up, it'll be fine with me, but we'll have to ask Jackie what her plans are."

"I normally take her and Emily when they're free, so we'll try to make it a foursome today. I'll check with you later." He quickly turned and was out the door so fast that it was as if he wanted to escape. Jessica was thoroughly confused as she'd watched him leave, but when she turned to watch the boys, she found Jackie watching her with a big smile on her face.

She just shrugged and then went over to some of the larger toys to make sure she understood what they were and how to operate them. *Someone with a lot of imagination certainly made the selections for this room. Had it been C.J., or Jackie, or had they hired a professional to help them with the furnishings and toys to meet the needs of several ages?*

It was hard for her not to watch as Darren and Warren had become engrossed with the pieces of a big wooden puzzle that Jackie had spread on the floor. The pieces were large and different shapes, some the size of bricks, others the size of 12"x12" floor tile, and still others in triangles, circles, and diamonds. There was actually a puzzle board cut in the wood of the floor, and the boys were trying to put the pieces where they belonged. It makes a picture on the floor when put together correctly. Jessica, feeling mesmerized, didn't see Jackie come to stand beside her.

"You look as infatuated as I did the first day I got to see this room. C.J. drew the plan he wanted, the areas for each age group, and the common area for doing things all together. It is the most thought out plan I have ever seen, and the kids seem to love it and really respect the toys that are here. I am so grateful for the opportunity to know C.J. and to be able to work with him.

I noticed the way he was looking at you earlier, Jessica, and I would say that he is truly smitten with you. Before you and Emily arrived, he couldn't keep from talking about you, explaining what has happened from the moment he saw you on the beach to the boat ride and even the problem with your boyfriend, which, by the way, troubles him deeply. I hope you don't mind that he shared that information. He's worried about your return to UNC and what that boy may try.

Do you feel you can handle the situation at school or should you ask for an escort for between classes? I hope I'm not being too nosey, having just met you, Dear, but I'm an old grandmother, remember, and that gives me some privileges." She started chuckling so loud that the boys stopped their play to watch her. "I'm sorry, boys, go back to your puzzle. I just got tickled at something Jessica and I were discussing."

"I can't find where this big round piece goes," Warren sort of whimpered. "Does it really belong in this puzzle?"

"Well, let's see. You two have really done a wonderful job of finding all the places to put those pieces, but there is one space I see that still calls for a big round piece. Look real hard and see if you can find it, and then I'll show you if you still can't find it. It's not exactly in the square where you've put all the others."

Knowing that it wasn't in the square was all the boys needed to hear. They started around the outside of the puzzle and both spied the big circle at the top simultaneously. "There it is," they yelled and ran to get the one big piece. They began to fight over which was going to carry it, but Jackie solved that by having each take hold of opposite sides and then placing it in the puzzle together.

"I want you to come and stand over here on the stage and look at the picture you created. Do you see something that doesn't look quite right?"

Looking very carefully, Darren said, "This looks like it should be a balloon, but it's not all there, and the one next to it doesn't make anything look right. I should've known we were making a picture when it was a puzzle. Are they all wrong?"

Warren then said, "This hand isn't right, but how come the pieces fit?"

"You have done quite well, but I think there may be three or four pieces that need to be exchanged. Do you remember how many pieces of each shape you started with?" Jackie asked.

"I think there were two," Darren answered and Warren quickly agreed. They quickly looked at the pieces that didn't match and realized they needed to exchange six of the pieces and the picture would be complete of a boy and girl holding balloons in their hands. They had big smiles on their faces as they looked at the corrected puzzle, and they both said "That was fun."

"Now that we have it all finished, the next fun part of it is to put the pieces all back in the box. It has to be done just right, so you bring me the pieces as I call for them. The first ones I need are the big squares." And so the procedure continued until all the pieces were in the storage box. As if it had been planned, just as it was finished, the door opened and C.J. entered with the parents.

"My goodness, didn't you play with anything?" asked the father in disbelief.

"Yes, Daddy, we played with a lot of things but you should've seen the big puzzle we put together right here on the floor." Darren pulled on his father's hand until they were at the space on the floor. Of course, Warren had taken his mother's hand and pulled her along so they could show both of their parents what they had done.

"See all the different sizes and shapes?" Warren

pointed out as he got down on his hands and knees to touch each different space. "There are pieces that go on each of those, and they make a picture if you put them all in right. We made a couple mistakes, but we found them and then saw a boy and girl holding balloons. We got to put them all back in the box, with her help, that is. We really had fun."

"I think your mother and I will have to take some lessons from Mrs. Olin," he chuckled, "but let's go now and get some lunch. Does that sound like fun, too?"

"Yes, Yes, Yes," they sang in unison, and the family headed for the door.

"Thank you so much for giving us a little time with each other," they whispered so only Jackie and Jessica could hear.

"Well, another grateful family," C.J. uttered, "so are you ladies ready for some lunch? I think you may have another sitting job this afternoon, but it'll probably be only to watch a little one sleep."

After locking the room, they walked to the office to pick up Emily and then the four of them headed for the deli. Jackie and Emily scooted into one side of the booth so it left Jessica and C.J. to share the other side. "After you, my lady," he performed as he made one big graceful sweep of his hand to guide her to the seat.

Jackie and Emily couldn't hold back their grins, and of course, Jessica knew what they were trying to do. *Well, I don't mind sitting beside their boss, but it makes it much more difficult to admire all his handsome features. It would seem rather obvious if I were to sit sideways and stare, though, wouldn't it?* She almost chuckled aloud as she decided to give the two conspirators a rather curt grin.

After they had given their sandwich and drink orders to C.J. who had volunteered to be their server, they told Emily about their morning. When C.J. was seated, after doling out their orders with all the flair of a well trained waiter, he asked Emily about the check-outs yesterday and this morning. He was trying to find a room for Jessica or should he proceed with fixing the room next to the playroom for her.

"Why can't she continue staying with me and we'll just get here as early as we need to each morning?" Emily exclaimed because she wants Jessica to be her house guest. She wants a friend and she feels Jessie would be a good one if all works out the way she'd like.

"You have a long enough day as it is, Em, and if Jessica is here at the resort, she won't have to get up as early and can get to bed more quickly when her day is completed. That is why, so don't argue with me. I've discussed the situation and the room with her, and she understands that sometimes we have a rather early request for a sitter and other times it gets later than it should before the parents get back. So, was there a check-out or not?"

With a half pout, Emily said, "Yes, the young man checked out of the small corner room with the twin bed because his friends arrived and they had made reservations in Surf City."

"All right, reserve that one for Jessica. If you want her to stay with you tonight, fine, but tomorrow night she stays here."

The rest of the lunch went well although Emily kept giving C.J. some of her rather disgusted looks until he, with a smile but in a most businesslike way, said, "Em, you'd better change that attitude of yours quickly or I may have to replace you. Understood?"

"Yes, Mr. Peterson, Sir." She wrinkled her nose at him, but she also gave him one dazzling big smile which said, "Your bark is much louder than your bite."

The afternoon was exciting as Jackie and Jessica not only had the little year old girl, who was asleep on her mother's shoulder when they arrived, but about an hour later, a little three year old girl was brought in who wanted to be read to. Jessica held her on her lap in the rocking chair, but before the story was completed, she was also asleep. With a little spare time, she and Jackie inspected the room and Jessica felt, after another day of instruction, she should be ready for Wednesday.

CHAPTER SEVEN

Jessica had planned to catch the bus Saturday evening and go back to school, but when she asked if Emily or C.J. would take her to the station, she was quickly informed by her boss, "You're not taking the bus back to school tonight, Jessica. Em has Sunday off, so right after the church service tomorrow, I thought the three of us would take off to see some of the sights along the shore and then we'll get you back to UNC."

"But, I can't impose on you to do that. You've already done too much for me this week, C.J. Just take me to the bus station. I can go back by myself."

"There's going to be no arguing about it. I'm ready to get away from here for a little while, and Em is always ready to go for a ride."

She still couldn't believe the exciting week she'd had after Todd had so completely ruined her trust in him. And, it had been the most wonderful few days. Emily had been able to spend several hours on the beach with her, she thoroughly enjoyed the little ones she had taken care of, and C.J. had gone out of his way to make her stay enjoyable.

They had taken a few long walks on the beach to watch the sunsets, and he had pointed out all the different types of boats out on the water. He had taken just the two of them again on his boat one evening, and he had invited her into his apartment to watch a movie Friday night.

The parents of a 4 year old boy, with whom she'd been sitting, had been delayed due to an accident which had closed the highway just north of Wilmington. After they'd called to explain their situation, C.J. had come to the playroom to keep the two of them company until the parents could return. He'd brought food and the little boy had gotten so tickled when he saw the big, tall man sitting on one of the little chairs at the table which is used for crafts, group reading, or snacks, but it wasn't long until C.J. had him sitting on his lap..

After they had eaten, C.J. was down on the floor keeping the little boy amused as they played with many of the toys which were soon scattered around the room. As she watched, Jessica thought, *it's going to take a while to put these all away, but he would make such a great father with a child of his own.*

The parents had returned about 8 o'clock, humbly apologized and then left to get their little one to bed. He had been so good, but was starting to yawn and get a little fussy just before his parents arrived.

After a little teasing, back and forth, as to who was going to put everything away, C.J. and Jessica worked together to quickly restore the room to order, and then C.J. asked, "Would you like to watch an old John Wayne movie with me tonight? It isn't that late yet and I've had this movie rented for over a week. I'll probably have to pay a fine when I return it."

"I'm not about to turn that down, Mr. Peterson, because John Wayne has always been a favorite actor of mine."

He'd taken her by the hand as they walked to his apartment, and they'd thoroughly enjoyed watching Maureen O'Hara tangle with the rough and tough hero. C.J. had popped some popcorn and gotten a couple of sodas from the fridge to make them feel like they were at a real movie, and then he'd slipped his arm around her. That had made her a little apprehensive, but it appeared his thoughts were totally on the movie. Even afterwards, when he'd walked her to her room, she'd thought he was going to kiss her as he'd hesitated at the door, but then he'd just smiled and said, "Goodnight, Jessica, I've really had an enjoyable evening," and then slowly walked away.

On Saturday, since there were no scheduled sitting jobs and they could be reached by cell phone if something came up that they were needed, Emily had gone with her to browse at some of the beach shops. She had picked up some mementoes and a cute shorts and top outfit, and they had returned to find C.J. waiting to take them on the boat. It had been a great ending to a great week.

Now it's time for me to return to college and try to finish the semester without any problems with Todd, Jessica thought when she awoke Sunday morning. C.J. had come to her room to take her to breakfast and Emily had arrived in plenty of time to have coffee and a big bagel with them before they went to church. Since Jessica had her bag packed and in C.J.'s car, they could take off as soon as the service ended.

His car was an older model, but it was in excellent condition, and it had a bench-style front seat so all three of them could sit together. Emily whispered to Jessica, "You'll have to sit in the middle because you're smaller (by about 3 pounds and 3 inches). Also, I always get claustrophobia when I have to sit between people in a small space like a car."

Of course, Jessica didn't believe her for one minute, but she was happy to sit in the middle and be close to C.J. one more time before her fairy tale spring break was over.

C.J. seemed a little quiet today, but Jessica was not going to dwell on it since she certainly doesn't know all his moods after such a short time. They headed north thru Surf City and to North Topsail Beach where they crossed over to the mainland and took Rt. 172 to Rt. 24 which took them to Morehead City. Unknown to the girls, C.J. had asked the restaurant to fix a picnic lunch of fried chicken, coleslaw in small containers for each of them, and a selection of fresh fruit. He'd been able to slip the cooler into the trunk and say nothing until pulling into the Ft. Macon State Park.

"Time for lunch," he'd announced as he parked, jumped out and proceeded to get the cooler out of the trunk and head for one of the picnic tables. Emily looked at Jessica, smiled as she shrugged her shoulders, and opened the door. "Come on, Jess and Em," C.J. called.

"Well, he got to the nickname before he got you back to school, anyway," Emily chuckled as they made their way to where he had the food on a plastic tablecloth spread over the table. He handed them a paper plate, plastic fork, and a paper cup as he held up a tall thermos containing lemonade. Plenty of napkins were available as well as towelettes for their greasy fingers. He sat across from them so he could see their faces and especially drink in Jess's beauty before he had to let her go. His grin couldn't be contained, as he watched them enjoy the food, because this was the first time in years that he had planned such an outing. After they'd finished eating, they'd decided to walk for a little bit around the park to help digest their lunch, and then ended up racing back to the table to dispose of all the paper things and the left over food. Of course, C.J. won the race with those long legs of his.

Back in the car, they headed toward New Bern,

where they stopped to watch the Neuse River for a few minutes, then on to Kinston, Goldsboro, Raleigh and then Chapel Hill.

He hadn't told Jessica that he and Emily both had gone to UNC so they knew the area pretty well. As he drove around the campus, however, Jessica spoke up. "I'm quite impressed with your vast knowledge of the campus, Mr. Peterson. Could it possibly be that you might have attended this college and just kept it under your cap? And, of course, Emily must've known, too, so I see that I have met two determined conspirators who want their backgrounds kept a secret. I guess I'll have to do some investigating so I can see just what kind of people I've been associating with this week and what you want to keep hidden."

"Oh, please, Jess, don't do that. You really wouldn't want to dig up all that bad stuff about me, would you?" He and Emily were both laughing as they left the campus and were soon on the road leading to Jordan Lake. He parked close to the water, and then they walked around for awhile to stretch their legs and enjoy the wonderful breeze coming in off the lake.

As they strolled along, he reached for Jessica's hand. She moved away slightly as she thought they had accidentally bumped into each other, but he grabbed her hand and pulled her back beside him. "Jess," he'd said softly as he'd stopped and turned her to face him, "I want you to come back to Breaker Beach after graduation, and if I may, I'd like to be here for you when you graduate. Do you think your family would mind if a stranger, at least to them, were to be here?"

Emily had moved away and was standing near the water because she wanted the two to have their privacy. She was silently praying, *Dear Jesus, I'm hoping that it will work out for them to be there for each other. This week, as I've gotten to know Jessica, I've felt so certain that she was led into C.J.'s arms by Your great love and knowledge. They have both experienced a tragedy in their lives, and it would be wonderful if they could encourage one another and build a future together. If I'm pushing myself into the plans You have for them, please forgive me. Amen."*

Jessica was shocked. "But, C.J., why would you want to make the trip for a complete stranger? All I have been is a burden for you and Em this whole week, and I wouldn't know if I could find a job if I did come back to the beach."

"We'll find something for you to do, Jess, if you'll only promise to come back and give us a chance. Maybe we could start a small pre-school right in the hotel if we can't find a building close by that is suitable. I just know that I want you to come back, so I'd like to come to the graduation and then take you back with me. If you want to go home first, we'll do that, too. Please, will you do this for me, or, at least, think about it?"

"But,"......She was speechless. *I know God has been with me this week, first saving me from Todd, and then putting me into C.J.'s arms and his life. But, is this all God's plan, or is it a rebound situation that I may regret later? I've realized throughout the week that my feelings for C.J. were becoming more than a close friendship. There is contentment when I am with him, and an excitement or desire to know more about him, both of which I'd never had with Todd, and that is very confusing to me.*

"C.J., I just don't know what to say because my life has taken such a drastic turn this week. Would you let me think about it for a few days and then call or write you? I've loved this week, I think it was one of the happiest times of my life, but I haven't really had a chance to think about my future since it was shattered by Todd just a week ago?"

"I can understand that, Jess, and I guess I'm being a little selfish to think you could go from a future you thought you had with Todd into a completely unknown scenario. Just remember, I'm not asking for a commitment from you because I realize we've just met a few days ago. We would definitely need more time to get to know each other, but I do know that you're the first woman I've even wanted to be close to since.....let's just say my junior year in college. Maybe I'll tell you the story some day if we can continue our new found friendship."

"I'll never forget the friendship we've developed in such a short time, C.J., and also getting to know Em and Jackie. I want to come back to the beach to see all of you, but I just don't know whether I can find my future there. It's sort of like I'm in a dream and I'll awake anytime now and be completely alone. I do understand that Todd is now gone from my life, though, and I could never consider spending time with him again."

"That's all we'll consider today, Jess. You let me know if I can come to graduation and what you'd like to do after that. I'll be waiting for your call or letter. We'd better get back, get something to eat and then we'll drop you off at the sorority. You were pretty lucky to have been chosen to stay as the student counselor your senior year. Let's go, Em," he called as he took Jess's right hand and walked toward the car.

"Please, C.J., don't be upset with me."

"Jess, I'm not the least bit upset with you. I've loved being with you this week, and it's the first time in such a long time that I've even wanted to be near a pretty girl." He chuckled as he ran his right thumb down her cheek and his fingers tenderly grasped her chin. He stopped and turned her toward him and then put his free arm around her back as he still held her other hand. He then just looked into her eyes and smiled, "I hope you don't mind, Jess, but I'm going to kiss you."

She was taken by surprise, but his lips were so soft and warm as they met hers, her only thought was that it had been much too short a kiss.

CHAPTER EIGHT

They had stopped at a little out-of-the way restaurant, and Jessica realized that he must really know his way around this town. They had a hamburger, which was excellent, fries, and a drink. The middle-aged waitress was joking with C.J. which made her very curious, but if he had been here for four years, going to college, she assumed that he'd investigated the areas surrounding college more than she had.

When they reached the sorority, C.J. insisted on walking her to the door. He had wanted to kiss her again so badly, so when she hesitated for a moment before opening the door, he took the opportunity to cup her chin in his hand and lightly brush his lips across hers. "I hope you don't mind, Jess," he said, "but I've wanted to do that for several days now, and the one earlier just wet my appetite."

"It's too bad you waited so long, Mr. Peterson, because those appetizers certainly aren't going to last until we see each other again." With a quick drop of her bag, she put her arms around his neck and then waited until he responded with his arms reaching around her and his lips taking full control of the situation. "There now, that was better, don't you think? Maybe we can see if we can do even better in a few weeks." Grinning, she picked up her bag and then continued, "I hope I wasn't too forward. I'd hate for you to think I'm like those other girls, but I can't thank you enough for everything you've done, and please drive carefully going back tonight. You'll hear from me soon, I promise. Goodnight, C.J." and she slipped into the house.

He wasn't sure how he got back to the car, but Emily was waiting for him to tell her the verdict of this week. He instead asked, "Do you want to stay in town tonight, Em, or should we drive on back to the resort?"

"Since we didn't make arrangements to be gone, we'd better get back to the resort. I may need all that time to get you to tell me how those kisses made you feel."

The sorority sisters were scattered around the room, some trying to study, some were watching TV, and others were almost asleep. When they glanced up and saw her, almost all of them jumped up from their seats and yelled, "Jessica, where have you been?"

One after another was talking and asking questions. "Todd has been here three or four times looking for you, and he looked as if he was scared to death. We thought you went to the beach with him. Did you change your mind, but then, where did you go? Really, didn't you go to the beach with him? Please tell us what has happened."

"It's quite a long story that I'd rather not talk about except to say that Todd and I are no longer dating. We discovered that we have some differences that cannot be corrected, and I'm a little surprised he was concerned enough to drop by. If he does come again, would you tell him that I'm back safely, I had a great time, and I would prefer that he stay away from me? If there aren't any problems that occurred around here that need to be discussed, I'll go to my room now and dream of my future." With that, she gave them a big grin. "Thanks a lot, all of you, for your concern, and I'll see you in the morning. Goodnight."

As soon as she was out of hearing range, one after another commented on what she had said and what could've happened during the week. "What was that all about? You mean to tell me she's dumping Todd Olsen--one of the most popular guys on campus? What in the world could he have done to deserve that? Where has she been if not with Todd?"

"Well, if I have a guess, it's something he did or tried that was against her Christian beliefs," one of the girls spoke up. "You know how diligent she is about her devotions and also her prayers; and we know some things Todd just thinks he's gotten by with."

"Yeah, I was really surprised when she finally agreed to go with him to the beach, but she told me he'd agreed to get a two-bedroom suite. Do you suppose?" another added.

"No, she looked too happy to have been compromised, but he could've tried and she could've disappeared along the beach someplace," another surmised.

"Oh, Girls, this is really a good mystery, and I hope we learn the answer before the semester ends and she graduates. We can't let her leave without knowing what happened this week. I just hope we don't have to wait too long."

Adding to the mystery, the door bell rang around 10 o'clock and about six of the girls went together to see who was there. From the light on the porch, they could see that it was Todd again, so they opened the door. "Todd, we're supposed to tell you that Jessica is back safely, she had a great time, and she would prefer that you stay away from her. She looked happy and relaxed, but went directly to her room. Have a good night."

"Thanks, I will, but Jessica isn't getting away with treating me this way, and I'll not be staying away because she belongs to me. I'm going to have her, one way or another, so you can tell her that." He turned and stomped away. "Who does she think she is, anyway?" he mumbled to himself as he walked back to his apartment. He was plotting what he could do to persuade her to come back to him. He didn't want to lose the one virgin he'd found, so he decided to call his dad and get his advice without telling him how he had acted at the beach.

When the girls told Jessica what Todd had said, she looked a little concerned but just asked if they could walk together as a group back and forth to classes for a few days. That was easy to coordinate and things were fine for a couple of weeks. She'd received a couple of notes from Todd, but nothing threatening. He'd only asked if she would see him so they could talk. She'd almost consented but her inner voice kept saying 'No' and she'd heeded it.

Then one night the phone rang. One of the girls answered and turned to Jessica. "It's for you, but it's not Todd." Thinking that C.J. may have gotten the sorority phone number, she raced to the phone hoping to hear his voice, but it was not C.J.

"Hello, Jessica, this is Raymond Olsen. I'm glad I caught you. Todd tells me you've been avoiding him since spring break and he is quite upset. I'd like your side of the story, if you please."

She remembered that he'd always come directly to the point, but she didn't recall him being quite so curt. "Mr. Olsen, I would rather not discuss the problem that caused Todd and me to stop seeing each other. We just discovered issues between us that could not and cannot be resolved, and I'd like it to be left at that."

"It's not that easy, young lady. Todd is my only son, and I will do almost anything to see that he is happy. He told me you wanted a two-bedroom suite on the beach so we got it to appease you. I'd told him that it was OK to have the two bedrooms for show, but he didn't have to use them both." His chuckle almost turned her stomach.

"And he tried to use his father's advice, Mr. Olsen, and that is why I left the hotel and will not consider seeing him or talking to him again."

"Well, I didn't know you were so....shall we say, pure. No wonder he wants you. A virgin is hard to find these days."

"Goodnight, Sir." She couldn't take anymore and hung up.

The phone rang again, the same girl answered who had before and recognized the same voice. She turned to Jessica who shook her head. "I'm sorry, Sir, but Jessica has left the room because she was sick to her stomach................ ......I said, she cannot, or will not come to the phone ....Well, I believe that's her decision.....................I guess that's up to you, Sir, Goodnight."

"Thanks, Cassie, you're a lifesaver. I owe you big time."

"He was obstinate, overbearing, and just plain rude. Who was he, anyway?"

"Raymond Olsen, Todd's father."

"Oh! Really? That must be quite a family. Good riddance, I'd say. Todd must be one of those kids who has been given everything he wants, and he doesn't know how to accept the word 'no'."

Jessica couldn't keep from laughing even though her heart was pounding up in her throat. *What will Todd try next? I've written to C.J. inviting him to attend my graduation, but what if Todd and his dad try something on Graduation Day? I'd better call C.J. and ask him not to come.*

She called the girls together and quietly told them about the scene with Todd, how she had escaped, and about being rescued by these people at the resort. It included her sitting with the little ones, going for a boat ride, and staying with Emily. They now had the answer to their mystery and they were so proud of their Jessica.

The next day harassments started as Todd stood about 30 feet away from the group of her sorority sisters and shouted, "What were you doing down on the beach, Jessica, that you couldn't let your parents know where you were? You see, I called to see if they knew where you were, but they said they had no idea. Were you so ashamed of what you were doing, dear, sweet, untouched Jessica, that you couldn't tell them your whereabouts?"

She smiled as she realized her parents had done exactly what she'd hoped they would do. She'd called them from the Beachside Resort, when she'd awakened after being rescued, and they were glad to hear that she was safe and away from the likes of Todd. Of course, the girls with her knew the story so just stood quietly and shook their heads.

After two days of harassments, she'd had enough. It wasn't fair to the other sisters in the sorority to be exposed to this, so she went to the campus police. The following day, he'd started yelling at her again, but this time he was arrested.

That night she called C.J., but when he answered his phone, she didn't know what to say. "Hello," he'd repeated, and then asked, "Is that you, Jess?"

She'd finally found her voice and responded with, "I'm sorry, C.J., but I don't think you should come to graduation after all. It's not going to be anything special and after it's over, I think I'll go home and visit for a few days."

There was a moment of silence at the other end, but then he came through loud and clear. "What's going on, Jess? You're not the type to be so excited about my coming one day and turn completely against it a few days later. Have you had trouble with Todd? Come on, Jess, out with it or I'm coming up tomorrow and staying through graduation."

She'd started crying but was able to tell him what Todd and his father had put her and the rest of the sorority sisters through. "I reported him to the campus police, and he was arrested this morning. He'll probably just be fined, which his father will pay, so he could be back on campus shortly and right back to harassing."

"I don't think it works that way, Jess. He'll get a warning, and if he's caught doing anything again, he'll be gone and his diploma will be, too. You did the right thing, and I wouldn't expect you to have any more trouble from him. If you do, will you please call me immediately? There are some steps I can take that will guarantee his departure."

The sorority sisters insisted on walking with her for the following few days, but since nothing was happening, they started taking shorter routes to their classes. It was almost immediate that she felt someone was following her, but she saw nothing. She'd assumed it was just her imagination. After two days of suspicions, however, she'd started noticing odd shadows or flashes of light crisscrossing from tree to tree along her path. She couldn't under-stand what was causing them, but when none of the others had seen anything out of the ordinary, she really became suspicious.

One afternoon after her classes, she had just reached the front door of the sorority when she heard something in the bushes near the porch. One of the other girls had told about hearing something out there the day before, but it had been later and too dark to see if anyone or anything was there. Since it was only 4 o'clock today, it was light enough to see well if anything moved. She opened the door and then shut it again as if she had gone in, but she stood quietly and waited.

About a minute had elapsed when a male figure

emerged from the bushes and darted across the front yard and onto the sidewalk where he began to walk as if he were just passing by. He'd made one mistake, though, because Jessica recognized the clothes as being Todd's. She called "Todd," and a surprised but scared Todd Olsen turned and glared at her before he started running as fast as he could go. Several days later, she learned through the grapevine that Todd had decided to receive his diploma through the mail. He apparently had made arrangements to take his finals early and had enough credits to graduate so he had left the campus.

God had again rewarded her for having faith that He would protect her through trials and also happy times. She called C.J. to tell him the latest news and to convince him that she really did want him at her graduation.

"I'm really glad to hear that, Jess, because I was going to be somewhere near even if you had told me not to come. I don't want you to be a possible target for something he may still decide to do."

"I'm getting excited about graduation, but I wish it wasn't another three weeks filled with cramming and finals. I'm afraid I have some big time studying to do before my finals start, and I'd better say goodbye and prepare for tomorrow. Goodnight, C.J."

"Goodnight, Jess, I'll see you soon."

CHAPTER NINE

The finals did have Jessica staying up late as she realized she had been so occupied with Todd and his father that she had let her studying slip. After she'd completed the tests, though, she was pleased with her grades as she'd placed in the top 5% of her class.

Now, Graduation Day is tomorrow and she is getting so excited because her parents, two sisters, one brother-in-law, and C.J. will be here soon, and she is so anxious for her family to meet C.J. and for him to meet her family. She remembered back when she'd introduced her parents to Todd and they hadn't been too impressed. Maybe, with their jobs, they'd been able to judge his character much better than she had, but she still wonders how they'll accept C.J.

She had made reservations for her parents and sisters, but when she'd asked C.J. if she could make one for him, he'd said it was taken care of. Of course, having gone to UNC, he probably knew which ones were close to the campus, and he was, after all, the owner of a resort. She had hesitated, however, when he'd asked if he could take them all to dinner tonight, but he'd been so persuasive she had finally given in. He'd said he would pick them up at the sorority at 6:30.

Her parents had arrived a little before 6 o'clock and were busy visiting with all the sorority sisters and the other parents who were there. About 6:15 Jodi and her husband, Richard Grady, arrived with her other sister, Jill. There was so much noise that she almost missed the doorbell at 6:30 sharp. C.J. was grinning when she opened the door and reacted to all the chatter by covering his ears with his hands. She asked, with a giggle, if he wanted to add his voice to the others, but he thought they'd better go as he had made reservations for 7 o'clock. He'd followed her into the main lounge while she rounded up her family. She tried to introduce them, but her dad, with a chuckle, motioned that they wait until they got outside.

They didn't quite make it to the door when they all heard "C.J., you big handsome whippersnapper, where have you been keeping yourself?" He turned to see a mother of one of his fraternity brothers hurrying to catch him and give him a big hug. "It's been ages since we've had the pleasure of seeing you around."

"Hello, Mrs. Rawley, it is really nice to see you, too. It couldn't be that one of your daughters is graduating this year, could it? I thought they would have all finished college since it has been a few years."

"Oh, C.J. you are such a flatterer. It would have to be a granddaughter if there was one graduating since only one was younger than your buddy in college. But, you know me; I love to be involved so I'm just volunteering tonight for the social time here. Are you staying or are you stealing one of our girls away?"

"No, we can't stay, and I guess you could say I am stealing one of your girls away this evening. In fact we need to be on our way because we have reservations for 7 o'clock. It was nice to see you again." He took Jessica's hand and quickly headed for the door. He didn't want anymore surprises of people knowing him or a slip of the tongue.

Once they were outside, C.J. apologized for not taking time to introduce them. "If I had, we would probably have been there for an hour because she would've had to know all about each of you and our reservations would have been gone." he chuckled.

Jessica proceeded to introduce her family and then he directed them to a long white limousine double-parked in the street. As she stared at him, he gave her that cute grin as he said, "I thought it was the only way I could get us all in one vehicle." He turned to her father and brother-in-law to ask if their cars were locked. When they nodded in the affirmative, he opened the door of the limousine and they were soon on their way.

Jessica began to think he was kidnapping all of them when the driver kept going away from all the restaurants with which she was familiar. However, she was aghast when they'd turned into the Governor's Club and she thought he had lost his mind. "C.J., what are you doing?" she whispered so only he could hear. "This is an exclusive private club, and I thought only members could use the clubhouse."

"We're not going to the clubhouse tonight, Jess," he had just finished replying when the limousine turned into a driveway leading to a most beautiful home all lit up like there was going to be a party.

"We're crashing a party?" she asked.

"No, Miss Hale," he chuckled, "they're expecting all of us. This happens to be my parent's home and also where I grew up. They wanted to meet you and your family so they insisted we have dinner as their guests tonight. So, come, one and all, and meet my family."

"You do like to keep secrets, don't you, Mr. Peterson?" She tried for a scowl except it quickly turned into a grin as she shook her head in disbelief.

He was chuckling as he assisted Jessica and Jill from the car and with one on each arm, he led the way to the front door which opened wide as they approached, and the most adorable couple was standing there to welcome them. Behind them stood a slightly older C.J. and you couldn't deny that they were brothers because they both had that cute grin, as did their father. All three were almost the identical height, with the same athletic build and hair color except for a few gray strands showing in the father's. His mother was possibly 5'3" with a very slim figure, very pretty brunette hair and expressive brown eyes.

Jessica had been trying to pinpoint the difference between the looks of the father and the sons, but not until she'd looked at their mother did she realize it was the eyes.. C.J. and his brother have their mother's brown eyes while the father has the Swedish blue.

Hugs were exchanged, as introductions were made, and they were guided into a large living room where hors d'oeuvres and soft drinks were waiting. "If any of you would like wine or a mixed drink, I'll be happy to fix it," C.J.'s father offered, but they all shook their heads and selected a soft drink. The conversation went smoothly as they discussed their different vocations, their interests, and even their beliefs.

It was amazing how compatible they were as they discovered that Jessica's father, Stewart Hale, was an Insurance Agent; her mother, Wendy, was a loan officer at a bank, and Jodi's husband was an attorney. C.J.'s father, Brian, and T.J., his brother, are both doctors and have a family practice together, while Jeannette, his mother, oversees the Antique Store her family has owned for many years.

T.J. proceeded to take Jill under his wing, whispering in her ear, "Two loners always have to stick together." He then said loud enough for all to hear, "You haven't said if you work, Jill."

She told how she'd always wanted to have her own Real Estate Agency, but for now she was working at the bank with her mother. As all eyes then turned to Jodi, she'd only hesitated a moment after she'd glanced at her husband and grinned. "I'll only be working at the bank for one more month because," she took a deep breath and then continued, "we've discovered that I'm expecting around Christmas and Rich wants me to stay home and take no chances this time."

This was news to Jessica and she jumped up to give her sister a big hug. "Why didn't you tell me?" She looked at her parents and then at Jill and quickly realized they were just as surprised as she was.

"No one knew until tonight," Jodi explained. "Since the miscarriage, we wanted to make sure everything was all right this time before we made the announcement. We'd just meant to tell our family, but the time seemed to be right. I'm sorry if it was inappropriate."

"What do you mean, inappropriate?" Brian's soft voice had a caring tone to it. "We family doctors love to hear about little ones making an appearance. We hope everything will go well this time."

It was 7:30 when dinner was announced and they headed to the dining room two by two. Jessica glanced at Jill and could tell that she was not the least bit disappointed to be coupled with T.J. She actually thought they made a nice couple with Jill's chestnut brown hair, her beautiful creamy complexion, and her sparkling brown eyes walking next to T.J. with his sandy-colored hair and dark brown eyes, a very nice complexion but not quite as tanned as his nautical brother. *He probably can't get out on a boat as often as C.J., but most likely spends time on the golf course. Whatever, they are really two handsome guys, and I'm curious why T.J. hasn't married. I remember Emily telling me that he had been her first love, so what had happened? I have certainly realized that I want to know a lot more about this very intriguing family.*

She felt a little nudge and looked up to see C.J. smiling at her. "You're off in a world of your own again, Jess," he whispered. "Something you'd like to share?"

"Sorry, I was just thinking about how nice it was getting to meet your family, but you should've told me how wonderful they are," she whispered back.

The ten of them fit nicely around the large table in the beautifully decorated dining room. Jessica had noticed, in the living room and now in here, that the Antique Store most likely had supplied a lot of the furnishings. Each piece complemented the others, and it was a delight to let her eyes wander around the room admiring the paintings on the walls as well as the antique dry sink, sideboard and china cabinet.

Jessica mentioned the painting over C.J.'s fireplace and how she'd always admired the work of Rembrandt. She then wondered if she should have mentioned it when C.J. looked at her with an odd expression on his face. "You'd never said anything about the painting before, Jess, so I assumed it didn't mean anything to you."

"I'm sorry I didn't mention it to you, but I did ask Em about it on the way to her place that night. Since I heard the story about it from her, I guess I forgot to say anything to you."

"That girl knows more about me and my family than anyone should, but I just wish she would keep some of it to herself so we could have the pleasure of sharing it once in a while with our friends," he chuckled.

Jodi and Jill had immediately realized that C.J. had given Jessica the nickname they'd tried to get started when she was little, but their parents had discouraged it. Jill grinned at her parents now and said, "Now, Mom and Dad, what are you going to say to C.J. about the nick name that you wouldn't let Jodi and I use?"

Chuckling, their dad replied, "A lot of years have passed since then, Jill, and now, if Jessica is comfortable with it, we will be, too."

"Why didn't you tell me that your folks wouldn't like me calling you Jess?" C.J. had teased as he gave her a little punch in the arm and then turned to her parents. "I'm sorry, I sort of give everyone I meet with more than a two syllable name, a nick name. If you'd like, I'll be happy to make an exception and call her Jessica, at least in your presence." He gave them his cute, devilish grin.

"We'll leave that up to you and Jessica. Whatever you decide will be fine with us," her father replied.

The evening had been exceptional and just like clockwork, when they stepped out on the large porch that appeared to continue around the side of the house, the limousine turned into the driveway. Everyone still had things to talk about on the way back to the sorority, and they'd also discussed the procedure of the graduation in the morning. They'd agreed on the approximate spot where they would meet her after it was over, so when they arrived at their cars, they said goodnight and took their leave.

Jessica turned to see C.J. still standing there, his hands at his side and his legs crossed at the ankles as he leaned against the side of the limousine. "Come here, Jess," he said in his soft sexy voice, and as she approached, he reached out his arms to enfold her and pull her close. He then tilted her chin with one hand while keeping a tight grip on her back with the other. Very quickly his lips reached hers, slowly moving his tongue across her lips softly and wanting so much more. He then returned to another kiss and felt the tingles, vibes, and desires he had known only with Peggy grow stronger than anything he had ever experienced before. He knew he had to walk Jess to the door, but how he'd love to hold her and kiss her for hours.

"It seems like an eternity since I got that kiss up there on the porch when Em and I brought you back after your spring break. I hope you enjoyed that one and these as much as I did, but now I'd better get you inside so you can get a good night's sleep before the big day tomorrow."

"Goodnight, C.J.," she whispered as she stepped back and watched him push away from the limo. As they walked toward the door of the sorority, her thoughts were troubling ones. *What is he really feeling? His kiss was so sweet and gentle and I know he could be the man of my dreams, but was he just being kind because he knows how much Todd hurt me with his actions. Does he just want me to feel loved during graduation? He has been so attentive, and he seemed so concerned about my struggle with Todd, but now he's taken my whole family to meet his. It's hard to believe he's actually for real.*

Her mind was racing overtime as her thoughts continued. *Are all the things Emily told me about his devotion to the girl who died really behind him? What about the fear his family had about his depression? There's also his own admission about being indifferent, and how he sometimes misjudges people who are trying to do the right thing. He's someone I'd like to get to know better, for sure, but what am I going to do when he starts talking about my returning to Breaker Beach again? How do I know he isn't another Todd?*

"Dear Lord," she silently prayed, "how I wish there was a verse that could give me the exact words

I need right now." Immediately she heard, "Trust in the Lord with all your heart; and lean not on your own understanding; in all your ways acknowledge Him, and He will make your paths straight." She couldn't stop her smile.

"Jess, I don't think you're with me right now, and I think you need to go in and get some sleep. It's been a long and somewhat disconcerting night for you, and you have a big day ahead of you tomorrow. I'm going to kiss you once more, and then I'm going to see that you go inside. I'll be here tomorrow to see you graduate and then help you make a decision."

Oh, how can that grin send so many chills up my spine? Then his lips were on hers and she could only wonder which was the most electrifying.

His arm had remained around her as he'd walked her to the door. "Jess, remember, I'll see you tomorrow," he said as he gave her a little push inside the house. He headed for the limousine with his heart thumping and his thoughts saying, *I think I Love You, Jessica Hale, Truly I do, but I'm still having trouble with my commitments.*

Jessica hardly noticed her sorority sisters as she felt she was floating up the stairs to her room. They were smiling and so thrilled for her after seeing that handsome guy who had come to pick up her whole family in a limousine. "Where did she meet him anyway? Is he the reason she was so happy when she came back from the beach? I wish we'd heard more of her story instead of Todd and his ugly harassments. She is so sweet and too good for Todd now that we know what he is really like. If he's lucky, he'll remember what kind of a girl he had and maybe let some of it rub off on him."

When she got to her room, Jessica turned to Proverbs 3:5-6 to read in its entirety the verse that had come to her earlier, and then she prayed, "Dear Heavenly Father, who has watched over me for so many years, I thank you. I haven't been the easiest of your children to guide, because I was so sure I knew what I wanted and I'm afraid I didn't listen when I should have. And now again, I'm a little hesitant to put all my trust in You even when C.J. came into my life just when I needed him and has been the rock for me to lean on. Please help both of us, Jesus, because I'm sure he has his doubts, too. I also pray that Todd will find his way to You because I want him to have a good life. I pray for the safety of my family and that the future will be full of joy and happiness along with the clouds that are bound to arise. May I have the faith to know that You are always there beside me. Amen."

After thinking for awhile about how tomorrow will be a Sunday much different than any other she'd experienced, sleep did come, but one of her dreams was a bit upsetting as it showed C.J. sitting in a graveyard and staring at a stone marked *Peggy, To Be Loved Always by C.J.* How was she to cope with that?

CHAPTER TEN

Jessica had gone through all the motions of getting through the processional and reaching her assigned seat, but her mind was nowhere close to listening to what was being said to begin the ceremony. She'd heard a few thoughts now and then, but she was otherwise in a daze as she desperately tried to decide what she was going to do with her life now that her schooling was over.

Earlier, before finding her place in line, she had seen her family come and find their seats, but she hadn't seen C.J. *Could he have decided not to come after all?* she'd questioned as she'd walked over to where she could look out over the gathering crowd. "He did promise he would be here so I must've just missed him." She was quietly mumbling to herself when she felt a pair of strong arms coming around her and a kiss being put on the nape of her neck.

She then heard, "Is Jess upset about being an alumna or does something else have her mumbling to herself?" C.J. had whispered into her ear and then kissed her cheek. "You were a little hard to find, Jess, since you weren't anywhere I'd expected you to be. But, isn't it about time for you to get lined up for the processional?"

"Oh...I guess...it is...at that," she had stammered and checked her watch as she'd then turned around to face him. She was so glad to see him, and she couldn't stop her arms from going up around his neck.

He'd initiated a good luck kiss, at least that's what he'd called it, and then urged her to find her place. "I'll see you when it's over. Don't stumble now while going up after your diploma," he'd chuckled.

So now, she's sitting here trying to listen to the program that she'd studied and worked so hard to earn the privilege to attend. Then, all of a sudden, she clearly realized what she really wanted was to be held in C.J.'s arms. *Is this the answer you've been trying to give me, Lord? You want me to go back to Big Breaker Beach and be near C.J.?* The applause rose for the introduction of the Dean of the College and interrupted her thoughts, but she decided to take it as God's answer, in the affirmative, to her question. A verse from Isaiah then came to her: 'Whether you turn to the right or to the left, your ears will hear a voice behind you saying, this is the way, walk in it.'

She glanced at the program and was glad she'd only missed the Invocation and the Chancellor's usual opening remarks. She sat up straight in her seat, happy with God's quick answer for her, and she was able to concentrate on the rest of the program during which her peers spoke and were great. When the time came for the diplomas to be handed out, she felt relaxed and elated that she had finally accomplished the goal she'd set for herself, and she knew that God had been beside her all the way even when she wasn't listening very closely.

It was so exciting to hear the names being called of her friends and peers of the last four years and then watch as they were handed that coveted piece of parchment and to hear the applause. When she heard *Jessica Lee Hale* announced, the emotions of the moment took over as tears spilled down her cheeks amidst the big smile that kept sweeping across her face. She glanced toward the seats where she had seen her family earlier, and there they were all standing and applauding. And, beside her father stood the tall, handsome C.J., who, of course, had that precious grin on his face.

When it was over, she'd hugged so many and wished them a wonderful future that she thought her arms were going to fall off, but then she'd hurried to the spot where she was to meet all the ones she truly loved.

C.J. couldn't wait for her to reach them, when they saw her approaching, so he came to meet her. He nearly ran the last few yards, quickly picked her up off her feet and twirled her around and around. When he put her down, she realized his lips were coming toward hers, and he claimed the kiss right there in front of God, her family and everybody. Actually, no one really cared because kisses were being shared all over campus.

They joined her family, who all had those silly grins on their faces. She could feel her face growing flushed as she wondered how her parents were going to reprimand her for such a show of affection in a public place. She looked at C.J., but he appeared perfectly cool, calm, and collected as he displayed that grin, put his arm around her and gave her a quick kiss on the forehead. She could've whacked him, but when she looked at her parents, they were still smiling. Her dad, clearing his throat, said, "Should we head somewhere to get some delicious refreshments? It's been a rather long, warm day and I, for one, need a very large cool drink."

"I know just the place," C.J. offered, and they were soon on their way to a fabulous restaurant which had an outdoor eating area shaded with trees, some tall flowering shrubs, and many of the spring flowers were also in bloom.

"This is absolutely beautiful, C.J.," Wendy commented. "We're so glad you were here to suggest it, and I hope you know that we're very appreciative of all you've done for our family and especially for Jessica at the beach and also here." Her smile was so sincere that it brought tears to the eyes of Jessica, Jodi, and Jill.

"I've always liked this restaurant and the way

they've enclosed this area with the live shrubs instead of a fence. Actually, I'm working on a similar plan at the resort, so you'll have to come and give me your approval when it's finished. Not that I want you to wait that long before you come to visit. Do you have your vacation planned for this year? Maybe I could entice you to come to Beachside Resort at Big Breaker Beach."

If that grin works on them like it works on me, my folks, and probably the rest of the family, will be making reservations very soon at the Beachside Resort, Jessica mused.

"And that brings me to another subject," C.J. continued. As he took Jessica's hand in his and started making circles in her palm with his thumb, he said, "I don't know if Jess, uh, I'm sorry, Jessica has had time to talk to you about me wanting her to come back to the beach. I have some plans that I think might work for a pre-school that could be, from what I've gathered, the fulfillment of a dream she's had for quite a long time. I would need her there for input and inspiration. I also want to get to know her better, such as her likes and dislikes, her background, and more about her dreams for the future.

She also needs to know more about me, my previous heartbreak, my family and my dreams. As you have seen me so freely demonstrate, I'm captivated by this young lady, but I can't very well pursue her, date her, and capture her love if she's hundreds of miles away. So, I'm asking you to help me convince her to come to Breaker Beach with me. I promise I will protect her, honor her and never let my emotions hurt her in any way."

Jessica had finally put her other hand over his to stop the chills that were sailing up and down her arm and spine from his thumb doing wonders as it massaged her palm. She was in awe of his straightforwardness about what he wanted, and she had seen admiration in her father and mother's eyes as they had listened intently to what C.J. was saying. She then glanced at Jodi and Jill, noticed tears in their eyes, and when she looked at Richard she saw a look of amazement. He had his arm around Jodi and pulled her to him so he could whisper something in her ear. She'd nodded and smiled as he'd kissed her cheek.

Her father, she knew, was desperately trying to control his emotions so he could reply to this appeal that C.J. had so eloquently made. He looked at Wendy, got a nod, a wink and a smile, and then turned his attention back to C.J. and Jessica. "Well," he began, "I thought the graduation was emotional and strenuous enough for one day, but this has topped anything I could imagine. Wendy and I were hoping to have Jessica at home with us for awhile after graduation, but it appears that God has opened a door that should not be taken lightly. As you know, C.J., it is Jessica's decision to make, however, and her mother and I can only give our consent and blessing to whatever she decides.

We really would appreciate having her come home for a few days so we could have a family reunion of sorts. She can then pack her belongings in her car, if this is her wish, and drive to Big Breaker Beach. Would that meet with the approval of both of you?"

C.J. turned to look at Jessica as he said, "You see, there are so many things I still need to learn about you. You've never told me that you had a car." That, of course, brought a big laugh from the whole family just as the server had arrived to see if they needed anything else. "I think we need to make a toast to the future, so would you please refill the glasses," C.J. remarked and then he took Jessica's hand in his again, which she had finally freed. "Jess?" he softly whispered as he grinned at her folks, "Does that sound like a good plan to you? I totally agree that you should go home for awhile, just as long as you consider coming to Big Breaker and giving my plan a try. We'll find a room for you at the hotel, or at Emily's, until you decide if this plan of mine is what you really want."

After her answer from God, it didn't take Jessica long to say, "Yes, C.J., I'll go home for a few days and then I'll drive to Big Breaker Beach and see what the future holds for me and my dreams." She smiled at him and also her parents when she saw the approval on both of their faces.

CHAPTER ELEVEN

W hat's your plan for the rest of the day?" C.J. asked as they were finally leaving the restaurant. "Do you have to get your belongings out of the sorority house immediately or can you take your time doing that?"

"I have almost everything in my car now. Since I only had clothes and a few personal items that I brought for my room, it wasn't a big deal. I have my computer, stereo, Bible, and purse still in my room, but that should be about it. I think I'm supposed to vacate by the first of the week, if possible, so they can start decorating. They can get started in my room before the other girls have to be out."

"I was hoping I could get you to stay over tonight so we could have a real date before we have to go our separate ways. Do you think Jill would stay with you and then you could have someone to drive home with tomorrow? You can stay at my folks' tonight, and I could call T.J. and make it a double date if you think Jill would want to see him again."

"You're really full of ideas, aren't you, Mr. Peterson?" she giggled, "but it would be fun to have a real date before I come down to the beach and it becomes all business."

He chuckled at that remark. "Are you suggesting that I'll become a stern, rather overpowering boss once you get back to the beach? Was I that disgusting before?"

"What's all this discussion about, if we may be so inquisitive?" her father asked as he and her mother caught up to them. "We thought we would head home unless you need us to take some of your things in our car. I think Jodi and Richard are ready to go, too. It's been a wonderful and most exciting day, but home sounds pretty good now."

"C.J. was just asking if he could take me on a real date tonight before we go different directions. He also thought if Jill would like to stay and maybe see T.J. again, she could be company for me on the way home tomorrow. He says we can stay at his parents' house tonight since the sorority asked if I could vacate my room this weekend."

"That would be nice for you to have company coming home, Jessica, but you'll have to ask Jill. I don't think she had any plans for tonight, but I'm never sure."

Jessica gave them both a big hug, thanked them for coming, and told them she would see them tomorrow. Her father and C.J. shook hands and C.J. then surprised Wendy with a hug. They headed toward Jill who was standing with Jodi and Richard. "Jill, would you be willing to stay here tonight and then ride home with me tomorrow? We can catch up on all that's been going on in our lives," she grinned. "C.J. says we can stay at his parents' tonight, and he'll call T.J. and we'll go on a double date. Would you want to do that?"

Jill looked a little surprised but she did remember T.J. remarking last night that he hoped to see her again real soon. *Could he have put this idea into C.J.'s head? I'd love to see him again.* "Well, I could probably do that, but how do we know T.J. will want to go along?"

C.J. couldn't hide that telltale grin, and Jessica and Jill both had to laugh. "Why didn't you just say that T.J. wanted to see Jill again instead of beating around the bush, as the old saying goes?" Jessica quipped. "Now I'm not sure you really want a date with me or if you are only doing it for T.J.'s benefit."

"And you'll never know for sure, will you, Jess?" he replied jokingly as he put his arm around her waist and gave her a little kiss on the cheek.

As much as she wanted to pout, she found it impossible to do when she'd rather be giving him a kiss, so she quickly stepped away from him and turned to hug Jodi and Richard and thank them for coming.

C.J. then extended his hand to Richard. "It was

certainly nice meeting you, Richard, and I hope we'll see each other again soon. Would it be all right if I gave your wife a hug? I never had a sister so it might be fun to see how that feels," he chuckled.

"Just be gentle with her, C.J., because she's carrying a precious little one now."

"Right, I'll definitely remember that." So, after a very tender hug and a little kiss on Jodi's cheek, C.J. then grabbed Jessica's hand and gave it a kiss, motioned for Jill to come along, and started for his car.

By the time they had Jessica's car packed and driven to his parent's home, they had just enough time to be shown the bedroom with twin beds that they were very welcome to use before Brian and T.J. got home from playing golf. When T.J. saw Jill, a big smile came on his face as he immediately headed toward her, wrapped her in his arms and then just proceeded to kiss her on the forehead, her cheeks, and then her lips. "Hey, Jill, I'm so glad we get to see each other again so soon. Are you going to give me the pleasure of being your escort again tonight?"

"So much for the bashful doctor," C.J. remarked and everyone had a good laugh except for T.J. and Jill, who seemed to be engrossed in another kiss.

"Is that the way I should've acted when I first

met you?" C.J. asked Jessica who was blushing and shaking her head negatively.

"If you had, in my state of mind that day, you would have probably never seen me again, but, I do believe you're making up for the slower start," she giggled. As he put his arm across her shoulders, he gave her a brief squeeze.

C.J. knew that his mom and dad were watching him closely and trying to determine if his attitude toward relationships had changed so quickly after meeting Jessica, or was he just putting on a good show because of Jessica's problem that he had shared with them. *I wish I could tell them all is well, but I feel, as much as I'm captivated by Jessica, I still haven't been able to shake a few reservations gnawing at me. I actually feel like I'm not only a little bit captivated, but very much in love with her, so why I'm still resisting becoming involved in a full-blown commitment, I don't know. I certainly enjoy the convenience of having someone to be with, other than Em, but I've also become used to having my independence after eight long years without Peggy. But, every day now it seems like that junior year moves further and further back into my past.*

After some snacks, they'd all freshened up a bit and then said goodbye to the guys' parents. Their mother had given Jessica and Jill each a hug and wished them a nice evening. When the four had left the house, Jeannette had a big smile on her face as she remarked to Brian, "They both seem to be such nice girls and their parents were so cordial, I hope we'll get to spend a lot more time with them."

"Don't get your hopes and dreams stirring up a wedding too soon, Darling, because you do remember what happened before in both their lives, don't you? God will bring the right girls into the picture when He is ready, and we need to be patient and wait for His lead."

"Oh, I know, Brian, but our boys just seem to be marking time, and I know they'd like much more than that. Did you see that look in C.J.'s eyes when he looked at Jessica? And what about that show of affection that T.J. showed to Jill? I don't know, Honey, but I think those Hale sisters may have the ingredients that both of our boys need. Do you see anything wrong with that?"

Brian chuckled as he watched the look of anticipation on his lovely wife's face. He pulled her into his arms and kissed her tenderly. "I love you so very much, Sweetheart, and

I pray that all your hopes and dreams come true."

Teasingly, T.J. had suggested that they take his sports car because it was so terribly embarrassing for a doctor to be seen in that old model Cadillac that C.J. drives. To even the score, C.J. suggested that they go

to the museum and maybe even the concert in the park before eating because he knew his brother was a stickler for dinner about 7 o'clock.

"That isn't fair, C.J. You're doing that just to get back at me for the remark about your car even though you know how long I drove my old Cad. My stomach will be growling, and I'll be famished as well as being embarrassed if we don't eat pretty soon. Did you guys eat after the graduation ceremony, so that's why you're pulling this on me, little brother?"

"We did have some appetizers but nothing too heavy, but we all had snacks at the folks, if you remember. What do you think, Girls? Do we let him have his way and eat before the concert? After all, the poor doctor has worked so hard trying to stay out of those sand traps and not make bogies today," he chuckled.

Jill turned around smiling, "I can hear his stomach gearing up already so maybe we'd better feed it. I'd hate to sit by a growling bear while I'm trying to listen to beautiful music."

They'd finally pulled into a drive-thru and gotten just enough to hold them until after they'd heard enough of the concert. The guys promised they'd go to a nice restaurant then and have a good nutritious meal. There wasn't time to visit the museum so they were driving around for a few minutes until it was time to go to the concert. C.J. had Jessica snuggled up against him and he'd realized just how comfortable and right she felt in his arms. He was also thinking that she hadn't asked for a single thing. She'd only seemed to be appreciative of what he'd done and had never expected anything more. But, could this be a very clever act on her part, and she's really reaching for the moon just like the others who have been actively pursuing him for the last five years?

Dear God, please help me before I do something to lose this precious bundle I'm holding in my arms, he prayed, and as he'd squeezed her a little tighter, he'd also remembered a verse that he had read in his Bible just the other day which said: "Do not judge, and you will not be judged. Do not condemn, and you will not be condemned. Forgive, and you will be forgiven." Luke 6:37

He'd turned in the seat so he could see her face and get in a better kissing position. He'd proceeded to tilt her chin and place his lips on hers, gently at first, but then he couldn't refrain from giving her all the love that was in his heart. He's definitely aware of feelings so strong at times that he wants Jess for his wife, but then the old doubts come creeping back in.

Even if I were ready to make a real commitment, how would I know she's ready? She may only be using me to get a pre-school started, and I know I've been a little too anxious to help in that area. Well, I have some time. She's coming to Big Breaker soon, and I'll be able to see just what Miss Hale actually has up her sleeve. I'll have to be just a little more careful and hold my feelings in check, but I'm sure she'll show her true colors before long so I can see what she really wants from me.

She's either a very clever manipulator or a wonderful Christian girl to whom I can finally surrender my heart. Whatever the future holds, I'm going to enjoy the concert tonight, hold her hand and hopefully steal a kiss now and then.

He wasn't expecting the Bible verse to keep haunting him, but 'Do not judge and you will not be judged' kept going through his head. *What does it all mean?* he pondered.

During the concert, C.J. glanced over at T.J. and saw that he was also enjoying the company of the new person God had brought into his life. *Could both of us finally put our pasts behind us and find true, lasting love with God at the center? I truly hope so, but my past experiences are still quite vivid in my memory when I really concentrate. I'm afraid I have a lot of praying to do to get my faith restored to the point that I'm ready to face the future and not look back.* But for now, he decided to squeeze Jessica's hand and give her a big smile.

CHAPTER TWELVE

After a great concert, they drove to a night club that had a small dance floor so they could hold their girls and look into their beautiful eyes. While they danced, T.J. had asked for Jill's phone number, promised to call her soon, and then he'd kissed her right there on the dance floor. With his cute grin and his attentive ways, he had Jill completely under his spell, but finally, after a wonderful evening, he'd pulled into the driveway at his parents' home. He took Jill's hand and led her to the swing on the side porch. "You and Jess can go on in, C.J., but I have some things to talk to Jill about and I'd like to do them in private. I'll see that she gets to her room in just a few minutes."

"Ordered as if he were giving a prescription to a patient," C.J. chuckled, but he took Jessica's hand and they walked to the back of the house and into a most beautiful garden area lit with low, soft glowing lights along the winding path, and several tall antique ornamental lights scattered around the area.

"Oh, this is truly a Garden of Eden," she whispered as she tried to see all the flowers and shrubs that surrounded her.

"I'm glad you like it, because I'm trying to find a way to have something like this at the resort where the guests can feel like they're someplace extra special." He stopped and turned her around to face him. "I'm hoping that you'll have some ideas for me because it's going to be a challenge to create a garden of beauty on the beach. Maybe I'll have to set you on a pedestal for the central attraction," he chuckled as he pulled her into his arms and gave her a kiss on the cheek. As they continued their walk, she discovered a lovely gazebo that was tucked in among the shrubbery. They sat there and talked about his plans, and she'd promised to be thinking of some things he could do to give it an ethereal elegance.

When they returned to the porch, T.J. and Jill were gone, but when they entered the house, the two were about half-way up the stairs. "Where have you been?" T.J. asked. "I thought you'd both be asleep by now." Turning to come back down, he quickly pulled Jill into his arms and kissed her lightly on the cheek. "I'll be talking to you soon, Jill. Be careful on your way home tomorrow." He then looked at C.J. and said, "I'll let you show the girls to their room, and I'll scoot on home. It's been a great evening."

C.J. escorted them to their room. "There is always

a nice selection of things to eat for breakfast around here so plan to have something before you leave for Sanford in the morning. Goodnight and sweet dreams, which I hope include two outstanding brothers," he chuckled as he headed on down the hall to his room.

Jessica and Jill awoke the next morning to bright sun shining in their windows. They were shocked that they had over slept so they hurriedly dressed and went downstairs. They were amazed by the number of items that awaited them when they reached the dining room. C.J. was sitting at the table, a cup of coffee in his hand, and the newspaper spread out in front of him. He looked up and smiled when they came into the room. "Well, I hope you had a good night's rest, sleepyheads, and are ready to tackle the drive home today. Help yourself to anything you'd like because everyone else has eaten and vanished. They said to tell you they really enjoyed seeing you and hope to see you again real soon. You're invited to stay here anytime."

"That's terribly sweet of them," they said almost in unison and then headed for the buffet. Everything looked so good, they probably went overboard, but they had the excuse that they wouldn't stop on the way home so would probably skip lunch. They looked at each other and started laughing as their plates were piled high when they went to the table.

C.J. put his paper down to inquire what they were laughing about, but he didn't have to ask. "Hey, I like girls who have a good appetite, and you two must run it all off during the day because there isn't an extra ounce on either of you."

"Thanks, C.J., but what are you buttering us up for? Is there a favor we can do for you in our little home town?" Jessica giggled.

"Nope, everything's hunky dory, but I may have to get a plate and join you. You've made me hungry again just watching you. Did you bring anything in last night that you'd like me to carry to your car?" he asked as he went toward the buffet.

"Everything is in this one little bag that we can carry out when we're ready to leave except for our dresses we wore yesterday. We didn't want to stuff them in with our pajamas. I'm really sorry we missed your parents. They've been so gracious to our family, especially to let us spend the night. We hope we can repay them someway.

"No problem. I think they miss the activity of all the guys who used to come home and spend the weekends with T.J. and me when we were in college. They really seemed to enjoy those years."

Even with a late start, C.J. had finished his second breakfast about the same time the girls had so when they were ready to leave, C.J. went out with them to see them on their way. All three saw the problem about the same time. The back tire on Jessica's car was very low. "I should've checked that when I filled the tank Friday," Jessica grumbled as she assessed the situation. "It has a slow leak so I think I can get to a station and then it'll be all right until I get home. I'll have Dad get me a new tire before I drive on down to the beach."

"I don't think I'm going to let the two of you drive on the highway by yourselves if this isn't the first time that tire has gone down. You wait until I throw my things in my car, and then I'll follow you home just in case there is any trouble."

Jessica kept fussing with him, of course. "That's not necessary, C.J. That tire has been acting like this for two years now. I just haven't wanted to bother Dad as long as it was staying up quite awhile after I'd put air in it."

"Just the more reason you shouldn't be out there on the highway without someone to help, so don't argue. I'll be right back out because I should get started home anyway."

"But there isn't a good route from Sanford," she still tried to argue, but C.J. was in the house before she could do anything except look at Jill and shrug her shoulders. He emerged again in less than two minutes.

They made it to the station and were soon on their way toward Sanford, and it was fun for Jessica to have some time alone with her sister. Jill will turn 25 in July, Jessica had turned 22 in January, and they had always been close growing up. They had spent one year in college together, and it had been a blast with lots of memories to last a lifetime.

They had been keeping their eye on C.J. and really did appreciate the comfort they felt knowing that he was following them, not too close, but that he was there if they were to need him. When they reached the edge of Sanford, however, they noticed that he had pulled a little closer so as not to lose them when they'd started making turns.

When Jessica made the turn onto their street, she let out an "Oh, No!" She'd seen a car parked along the curb, about two houses from their home, and had recognized it as Todd's. She'd thought about driving on down the street, but when she saw Todd sitting in the car, she decided she might as well face him here rather than have him chasing her all over town. As she turned into the driveway, she saw him get out of his car and start running toward her and also yelling. Jill jumped out quickly and headed for the house, telling Jessica that she was going to call 9-1-1 just in case. They didn't know if their dad would be home or not.

C.J. turned the corner when Todd was almost to Jessica and had just reached out to grab her arm. He saw she had escaped that try as he pulled on past the house and parked. He didn't know for sure who this was, but he thought it was probably Todd. He was out of his car and headed toward them on a run until he saw a gun in the guy's hand, which he was now waving erratically.

"Dear God," he prayed, "this kid has gone berserk. Please keep Jess safe and give me the knowledge and strength to do whatever is needed to help."

As quietly as possible, he had slowed to a walk toward them, trying to stay calm and keep his emotions in check, but he could only think how he would like to strangle whoever this idiot is. He was fairly close now and could hear Todd ranting and raving. "You belong to me, Jessica, and if I can't have you, nobody is going to have you. I've had to wait for a year and a half for you to come to your senses, and I'm not about to let you go now."

Just then the front door of the house opened and Jessica's father came out onto the porch. Todd turned to look at him and yelled, "Get back in your house, Mr. Hale, or I'll have to shoot you, as well as Jessica, if she won't come with me. I'm going to have her as my own, or nobody is." Turning back to Jessica, he continued on his rage and kept trying to reach her. "Those lousy campus police you reported me to aren't around today, Sweetheart, so I can be here legally to claim you." He reached for her once more, but she was able to back away.

"Ta..od," she stammered, "pl..please pu..put the gun dow..down and let's ta..talk."

Laughing now, he snarled, "I've got you a little

scared, haven't I, Sweetheart? You don't have your sorority sisters to protect you today, do you?" He then raised his voice a little louder as he stared at the house and waved the gun around as he screamed, "your dad had better get back in the house."

Todd was just bringing his gun hand down to an aiming position when C.J. suddenly saw the opportunity to act. He grabbed Todd's right arm, which was holding the gun, and brought it down quickly so the gun was pointing to the ground. However, as he tried to reach Todd's other arm, he heard the gunshot and then felt a pain shoot through his left leg.

"Now, Kid, what'd you go and do that for?" he moaned, but he kept a tight grip on Todd's right arm. At that same moment, Stewart Hale jumped from the porch and grabbed the gun as Todd stood somewhat in shock. C.J. released his grip on Todd's arm and slowly slumped to the ground just as the squad car arrived. Two officers handcuffed Todd as he continued to talk incoherently about how he was just claiming what belonged to him.

Jessica was on her knees beside C.J., who was now sitting on the ground inspecting his leg and the damage that had been done. One of the officers came over to them, and after checking the wound, asked if he should call an ambulance or would someone be able to take him to the hospital's ER.

Jessica assured the officer that they would take him to the ER. She was hugging C.J. and kept repeating, "What if something worse had happened to you? You weren't supposed to be here. I can't believe you risked your life to keep me from getting hurt. I love you so much, C.J."

"Hey, it was all worth it to hear those words. Just remember, you can't take them back," he tried to laugh but a sharp pain caused him to moan instead.

After Jill had come with a damp cloth and wiped the blood away, the officer applied a large tourniquet type bandage and said he would meet them at the hospital as soon as they had Todd delivered to headquarters.

"We'd better get you to the Emergency Room, C.J., and find out what damage the young fool did to you," Stewart said. "I was so afraid for Jessica when he started swinging that gun the way he did, but I saw you coming up behind him and knew you had the better position if I didn't give you away or cause him to start shooting. I just wish I could've done something to prevent you from being shot, or that the officers had answered Jill's 9-1-1 a little sooner."

They carefully helped C.J. up from the ground and he limped over to Stewart's car. He asked if Jill or Jess would get the keys from his car and lock it. Stewart then drove, but C.J. wondered if Jessica's dad was more upset than he was.

Luckily, the doctors discovered that the bullet had gone into the hard muscle on the inside of his left calf. It had neither hit a bone nor the large blood vessel so they'd be able to remove the bullet without too much trouble. And, since it was his left leg, C.J. figured he could still drive on home. The surgeon and the police had different ideas on that plan, however, so Jessica just smiled and said, "You're going to be our guest tonight, Mr. Peterson, and I'll fix you a big breakfast in the morning although not like the one we had this morning."

"After just telling me how much you love me, Miss Hale, you're now going to call me Mr. Peterson? Come here, you little troublemaker, and show me how much you really love me. I need a nice long affectionate kiss."

"But there are people watching, including my dad," she whispered, "and you have to go to surgery."

"And I don't think any one of them will care one bit if you give your rescuer a kiss before he goes to surgery. Do you realize this is the second time you have been rescued by me? I do love rescuing you, Jess, but I'd prefer it not becoming a regular habit if it's going to get more violent each time," he chuckled as he pulled her to him and got the kiss he'd asked for right there in the busy Emergency Room while he still lay on the gurney.

Jessica couldn't sit still and had been pacing all over the waiting room. "Jessica, Sweetie, please come and sit down. C.J. is in good hands, and it isn't a case of life or death, you know. We should be thanking God for sparing all of our lives today."

Jessica tried to give her dad a smile as she went over and sat beside him. "It's just that I feel so responsible for him getting hurt. He wasn't supposed to even be here, so I know it had to be God's plan that my tire was low this morning which made him decide to follow us home. I don't know what would've happened if he hadn't been here," she sniffled.

"I wondered why he was here, but I certainly was glad to see him coming toward the scene when Todd threatened to shoot me as well as you if I didn't go back in the house. I didn't dare move with him being so irrational." He patted her hand and then picked it up and held it hoping it might calm both of them.

It wasn't too long until C.J. joined them. The surgery had gone quickly and well, but he was asked to return in the morning so they could check for any possible infection. After the police had come and taken their statements, Jessica and her dad got him back to the house and comfortably situated on the couch before Stewart went to the den to work. Jill had gone to the bank to see if she was needed so Jess and C.J. watched some old movies until they both dozed off from the trauma they had just been through.

CHAPTER THIRTEEN

C.J., Jessica, and Stewart attended the arraignment the next day. Todd's parents had driven down from Durham to be with their son. His father had looked accusingly at Jessica, as if he were blaming her for his son being in trouble again. His mother, however, looked ashamed, sad, and somewhat lost.

When Todd arrived in court, he was still jabbering about Jessica belonging to him, and then he saw C.J. sitting beside her. He started struggling with the guards as he was trying to point toward C.J. as he shouted, "That's the one who should be arrested because he's trying to steal her away from me. He's just a thief. She wouldn't give me what I wanted, but she's probably given it to him because he's most likely a real smooth talker."

The Judge rapped his gavel and ordered, "The defendant will be seated and there will be order in the courtroom." When the one policeman was testifying about what he and his partner had encountered at the scene, Todd started yelling again that they were all liars. He was just claiming what belonged to him. His parents were completely shocked and couldn't believe this was their son.

The Judge warned Todd to be quiet or he would be removed from the courtroom. The policeman ended his testimony, and then the Judge asked C.J. if he would come forward and relate what he and Mr. Hale had done to subdue Todd and how he had gotten shot in the leg. When he had finished, the Judge also asked what his relationship was with Jessica Hale.

"I'm a very good friend to Jessica, Sir, and I came to attend her graduation from UNC Sunday. I then asked Jessica and her sister, Jill, if they would attend a concert in the park with me and my brother Sunday night. They spent the night at my parents' home and then, because Jessica's car had a low tire yesterday morning, which she told me was from a slow leak, I elected to follow them home just in case they had any trouble."

"Do you feel that Todd deliberately pulled the trigger on that gun to hurt you or possibly one of the others?"

"I don't think Todd really intended to hurt anyone, Your Honor. He had just become irrational and very confused because he'd felt that Jessica was going to be his wife one day, and when he saw that slipping away, he sort of lost it."

"You're very considerate and forgiving, Son, with a gunshot wound in your leg and all the verbal abuse he has aimed at you."

"I don't want to cause anymore trouble for him or his family. I only hope that he'll get some help so his life can be full and prosperous."

"Thank you, you may be seated." He then asked Jessica to step forward. "You seem to be the main reason that we are having a hearing this morning, Jessica. I'd like to hear your thoughts about why you think Todd acted the way he did yesterday."

"It's hard for me to realize that this is the same Todd I'd dated for almost two years, who had always been a considerate and generous date, taking me to meet his parents and talking about marriage once he got settled in business with his father. However, over our spring break, he asked me to go to the beach with him, promising to get a two-bedroom suite. We had the suite, but he then demanded to have things I refused to give, so I left early in the morning when I was sure he would be asleep. I walked for hours, very confused, shocked and angry until I started to collapse on the beach. C.J. and several of his staff rescued me, and we've all become very good friends.

Yesterday, he rescued me again, when Todd was threatening with the gun, and I feel very indebted to him, but I've also asked God to help Todd so he can work with his father, which has been their dream for years. I can only assume that Todd wanted more overall control in our relationship than I could give, and when he couldn't have his way, he simply couldn't handle it."

"Thank you, Jessica, you may be seated."

Turning to Todd, the Judge said, "Well, Young Man, I think you owe a lot to C.J. and to Jessica. Because of their testimony and wish for you to get help and again become a good citizen of our country, I'm going to allow your parents to take you home with them today. If, however, their promise to see that you get the help you require is not honored, I will then sentence you to 60 days in the Mental Hospital in this area. I really think you need the support of your family and it will be easier if you are in a hospital closer to your home. I'll be checking your progress with the hospital, where your parents have indicated they will take you, so I sincerely hope you'll cooperate and get well soon. This case is closed."

Todd's parents came over to where C.J., Jessica, and her father were standing. It did appear to be difficult, but Mr. Olsen extended his hands to Jessica and C.J. and, with tears in his eyes, said, "Thank you both. I was so afraid you had completely turned against him. I'd never realized he was so hyper, and we'll definitely see that he gets help."

Jessica gave him a hug and said, "I know you will, Mr. Olsen, and I wish all three of you God's blessings."

His mother stepped forward and embraced Jessica as tears streamed down her cheeks. And then, completely shocking her, she whispered, "I was hoping you'd be the daughter I was never able to have."

"I'm sorry, Mrs. Olsen, I've enjoyed meeting you and visiting in your home, but the future just didn't work out for Todd and me."

It was getting close to lunch time when they emerged from the courthouse, so they decided to get something to eat at a nearby restaurant before letting C.J. head back to the beach.

C.J. had seen the doctor early this morning and was given the OK to leave as long as he had the doctor close by at the beach. He reached for Jessica's arm and turned her to face him. He didn't hesitate to lean down, tilt her chin up so he could look into her beautiful eyes once more, and then give her a wonderful, although rather short, goodbye kiss. Taking her hands in his, he said "Goodbye for now, Jess. I'll be anxiously looking forward to seeing you at the beach. Please don't make me wait too long." He had that special grin on his face as he brought her hands to his lips so he could give each one a farewell kiss.

"It's hard to say goodbye, C.J., but I promise I'm coming back to Beachside Resort as soon as I have a nice reunion with my family, get a new tire, and figure out what I need to bring with me. My car probably won't hold all I think I'll need," she giggled.

"Don't try to bring too much to start off with. You aren't that far away so you can get things as you need them," he said as his fingers stroked her cheek. He then turned and shook hands with her father. "I hope our next meeting will be a little more calm, Mr. Hale." Then, with a chuckle, he got in his car and pulled away.

Jessica had tears in her eyes as she turned toward her father. He lovingly put his arm around her shoulders as they headed for their car. "He is quite the young man, as you already seem to know, and your mother and I would be very pleased if he becomes the one to win your heart. I've noticed, however, that both of you are struggling with some issues although you try to be so congenial. C.J. may even go a little overboard with his affection at times to cover up something that is bothering him. Do you want to confide in your old nosey father, or is it something the two of you need to work out together?"

"How do you do that, Dad? You've always been able to sense when things aren't quite right, and now you've done it again."

"Just the wisdom of being a father," he laughed.

"Well, to answer your question, Emily told me some things about C.J.'s past that he is still coping with. He hasn't opened up to me about them although he did mention not long ago that he might tell me some things if I returned to the beach and we could become a little closer.

You see, Dad, he lost his first and only love to meningitis when he was a junior in college. He finished his schooling but became indifferent to life until he heard about the Beachside being for sale, and he's spent the last five years making it an outstanding resort. Emily grew up next door to him and apparently also had a bad experience with a guy. So, when C.J. asked if she'd help him get the resort going, she went to the beach with him hoping it would help both of them. They have a wonderful relaxed relationship, and they are both Christians. My problem, if I have one, is not how I feel about him, but wondering if he can transfer his love from the memory of Peggy to someone else, like me. Of course, I'm still a little concerned about Todd and what he may decide to try if the treatments don't work. It might be well that I'm not going to be here. If he doesn't know where I am, he can't do any harm."

"Jessica, My Love, thank you so much for sharing that with me. I see that you're going to need a lot of patience if the two of you are going to have more than just a close friendship. I believe you have that already, even though you haven't known each other very long, but building on that so you can have a lifetime commitment is going to take an extreme amount of understanding, good communication between the two of you, and a desire to please each other in all phases of life. Your faith in God and a lot of prayers will be your strength, and I sure hope neither of them falters as you start a new chapter of your life. I understand the remark about his heartbreak a little better now, and I can pray for a special healing."

"Thanks, Dad, you have such good suggestions, and I do intend to keep my faith strong so my future is sure to be bright." She gave her dad a big hug as they got inside the house. "Are you going to the office this afternoon or are you working at home?"

"I'm working here unless I get a call, so if you need me, you'll find me in the den. What are your plans?"

"I'm going to start looking through my room to see what I want to take with me, so I'll see you later." She hurried up the stairs to start her selection, but of course, her thoughts were on C.J. She prayed that he would have a safe trip to the beach and no further trouble with his leg, and she was also able to include a prayer for Todd that his future would be fulfilling.

CHAPTER FOURTEEN

C.J. had called Emily to let her know some of the things that had happened and to also tell her that he wouldn't be getting back until around 5 o'clock. "I probably won't see you until tomorrow," he'd said, but when he'd walked into the lobby, there she was sitting and waiting. She jumped up and quickly followed him into his office.

"C.J.," she nearly screamed, "what in the world happened up there? Are you really all right, and how in the world is our little Jessica? I knew that guy acted weird when he came here that Sunday afternoon, and the stuff he's pulled since then has proven me right. Come on and give me the scoop on this so I can tell you my good news."

"Would you like to go first, Em? I'm ready to listen to your exciting story."

"No, no, no! I have to know all the details of this episode. My news can wait."

C.J. knew he couldn't get by with just a few details

with Emily, so he leaned back in his chair, gave her that cute grin, and told her everything that had happened--starting with the dinner at his parents, to the graduation and the double-date, (at which she squealed because she really wants T.J. to be happy again). He told about the big breakfast the girls had eaten, the low tire on Jessica's car and his decision to follow them home to Sanford. "Isn't that enough for now, Em?" as he glanced at his watch and realized it was almost time to eat. "Oh, I get it, you are deliberately staying late so I have to buy you supper. You've had to cook for a few days and now you want a free meal. Okay," he chuckled, "we'll go eat and I'll tell you the rest of the story."

When their order had been taken, he continued by telling her about the struggle with Todd resulting with the shot in his leg, the visit to the hospital, staying at Jessica's last night and the court hearing this morning.

"Now, you have every little detail of my weekend, and I'm sure you're thinking that I've fallen head over heels in love with our little Jessica, as you called her, and you could probably be right, but you could also be wrong. You know I still have my doubts about anyone who gets too close to me, but Jessica hasn't been anything but a good friend. But I did forget to tell you that she told me she loved me very much, when I was sitting on the ground with the wound in my leg, and I told her that she couldn't take it back" He chuckled as he looked at Emily who was, of course, grinning from ear to ear. "What's that big grin on your face all about?" he asked..

"I'm just so happy for both of you, and I hope it's the start of something very big, exciting and the wearing of white," she giggled.

"Don't get ahead of the game, Em, because I think Jessica may still have an issue or two that she needs to come to terms with, and my feelings are still going one way and then the other. I'm not planning to push toward any marriage until we have a chance, at least, to learn a lot more about each other, so I want you to take it one day at a time, also. I don't need any matchmaking ideas popping into your head. After all, we haven't known each other long enough for any long term license to be signed."

"Yes, Boss," she chuckled. "But now, let me tell you about one of our new guests in a one bedroom business suite who asked for an open end to his stay. He's an architect, who has his own firm in Wilmington, but who started working yesterday at the church we attend. They are apparently planning to add an addition, or a wing, to the building which will include a larger fellowship hall with the old one being turned into more class rooms, a library, and... and...a kindergarten. Isn't that just fabulous? He knew they already had one teacher, but he also thought that they're planning to have two or maybe three classes. He is so nice, C.J., and we had dinner together last night. It was wonderful!"

"Oh, Oh," C.J. let out a sigh. "No wonder you're thinking about wearing white and all that romantic stuff. And you haven't had to cook your own dinners, after all."

"I did cook except for last night, and it's a little early for dreaming, but he does really fit the qualifications I'm looking for." She smiled as she felt her cheeks heating up even in front of her friend who-knows-all-her-secrets. "In fact," she continued, "he came in about 4:30 this afternoon, and since I was there waiting for you, he sat down and we talked for a few minutes. Before he left, he asked if I would have dinner with him again Friday night. He's afraid he'll have his nose in his drawings the next two or three nights." She couldn't keep from giggling, and C.J. had to admit she was radiant.

"Well, then, my dear Emily, could I have the pleasure of escorting you to your car tonight, or would you like to keep me company for awhile? I think it's time for me to get my leg elevated and relax a little."

"Is your leg hurting quite a bit? Maybe we should have Chet come look at it after you've driven all that way." She slid out of the booth and waited as he took care of the tab.

"No, Sweetie, I'm fine. I'll check in with Chet tomorrow. I need a few minutes to call Jessica and then we'll get ourselves comfortable if you're sure you're not in a hurry to get on home."

"It'll be my pleasure, Boss, but do I get to listen to your conversation with Jessica as part of being your companion tonight?"

"Don't push your luck, Em. Some things are off limits, even to you, my long-time nosy friend and confidant."

His call to Jessica was the highlight of his day. Her voice sounded relaxed and he thought she really sounded happy to hear from him. He told her a little bit about the news Emily had given him and she reacted with an excited squeal. She would visit the church and find out more when she got there. He wanted to ask her when that was going to be, but he'd promised himself that he was going to leave that up to her. He sent his regards to her family and then joined Emily to watch a movie she had turned on. During the commercials and other breaks, she caught him up on the capacity of the Resort, which apparently was still full. He was glad to hear that, but then he brought up the availability of a room for Jessica when she comes.

"Do you know for sure when that will be?" Emily asked. "We'd hate to hold a room empty if she isn't coming for two weeks or more. We do have to think of business, you know," she grinned. "But, when she comes, I want her to stay with me until she finds a job and has an income. If I know Jessica, she's not going to take charity from you."

"That's so true. She's an independent one, that's for sure. Of course, I could ask her to share my apartment and my bed," he remarked and then heartily laughed.

"You'd better laugh after that remark, C.J. I don't think I'll even mention you said that or we might have her running right back to her home real quick like. That reminds me, what about T.J.'s date? Was she a friend of Jessica from school, or did T.J. come up with a date all by himself?"

"I guess I didn't tell you all the details, did I? He met Jessica's two older sisters when we were at the folks Saturday night. The oldest, Jodi, is married to an attorney and they are going to have their first baby in December. Jill is 25, and while Jessica looks a lot like her mother, Jill has her dad's medium brown hair and brown eyes but a nice build much like her little sister, Jessica. She's a couple of inches taller, actually about your height.

She and T.J. got along quite well that night, so he put me up to asking the girls if they would stay after graduation and attend the concert in the park with us Sunday night. The folks, of course, readily agreed to let them spend the night. T.J. appeared to really enjoy his time with Jill and secured her phone number before he went home. She works at the bank with her mother right now, but she has the dream of owning a real estate agency someday. Maybe T.J. can talk her into helping Mom with the Antique Store. I guess it would depend on what she likes about the real estate business. If it's seeing and showing people how they can decorate different homes, for instance, the store would be a great opportunity for her, and Mom could certainly use the help."

"Now who's getting ahead of the game?" she laughed.

"I guess I am, but my mind isn't working too well anymore tonight. I know it's not too late, Kiddo, but I feel like I've had quite a day, so if you don't mind, I'll see you to your car and then I'm going to see how my own bed feels. Did you see much of that movie?"

"Just enough to know it wasn't very good, but you don't need to walk me to my car, C.J. You need to get yourself to bed."

"You know me better than that, Em, so let's go. I'll call you in a few minutes to make sure you're home safely."

When Jessica had finished talking to C.J. her heart was pounding so hard that she had to talk to someone. She went to find Jill but she was in the shower, her mom was busy in the kitchen, but she saw her dad sitting in the den reading, so she slowly approached him. "Dad," she said and then hesitated until he gave her his attention, "could I talk to you for just a few minutes? C.J. called and gave me some news that I really have to share with someone."

"Of course, Jessica. I assume C.J. made it home all right, so come sit down by me and tell me what has you so excited you can hardly stand still." He laid the papers down that he had been reading and gave her his full attention. That was something else she had always admired about her dad. If one of his girls wanted his attention, they almost always got it.

She quickly told him what C.J. had told her about the church planning this addition for several reasons, one being that they wanted to start a kindergarten with possibly two or three classes. She could see the smile starting around his mouth and climbing to his eyes.

"Isn't it amazing how God works miracles in our lives?" he asked. "Your mother and I were so concerned about you going to the beach, and when you called and told us how Todd had acted, we almost panicked.

But just think what that has led to. There's C.J., a gentleman if there ever was one, who has become at least a best friend, possibly a job you've dreamed of for years, and a great place where you can enjoy the ocean that you have always been fascinated with. I'm so happy for you, Sweetheart, and I hope all your dreams come true." As he gave her a big hug, Wendy called them to the table where the news was reiterated again, and it was agreed that she was a very, very lucky girl.

CHAPTER FIFTEEN

For the next day or two, while the rest of the family was at work, Jessica tried to keep busy by going through most of her clothes to see what she wanted to take with her and then accumulating them into one spot with the other items she'd decided she would also want to take along. Her Bible, of course, was the first thing she picked up and ended up reading for over an hour. She smiled as she'd turned to the book of Acts and read how the apostles had endured so much that we might have the story of Jesus and His love for us. She thought of the events of the last few weeks and wondered what would have happened if she hadn't had Jesus and His strength beside her.

As she put her radio/CD player beside the Bible, she began to wonder where she was going to put these things since she had no idea where she was going to be staying. She soon became a little panicky as she couldn't realize why she hadn't given some thought to this. *I can't expect to just show up down there and be taken care of. Oh, Jessica, what have you been thinking? You don't have the money to rent an apartment without a steady job lined up.*

She sat on the edge of the bed, her head in her hands, and started crying.

"What's troubling my little girl now, just when we thought everything looked so good just a day or two ago?" her father asked as he came into her room. "You surely aren't that sad about leaving your family, are you?" he chuckled.

"I'll miss you all a lot, but that's not what is bothering me right now. I just realized I don't have a place to stay or a job when I get there. The job at the church probably won't start until next year if they wait for the new building to be finished. Oh, Dad, what am I going to do?"

"Don't worry about those things, Sweetheart. God has brought you this far and He'll see that things work out. Didn't you mention something about C.J. wanting to help you get a pre-school class started at the resort if nothing else showed up?"

"He had mentioned looking around for a building close to the resort, but since the church is going to start a kindergarten, he's probably given up that idea."

"Well, you can find something to do for a few months, even if you have to clerk in one of those beachside shops," he chuckled.

"I *can* do that, can't I? I have a business degree

so I should be able to take money from the tourists and put it in a cash register. Thanks, Dad, you could always come up with an answer for my dilemmas."

"Since that's settled, I have a couple of hours free this afternoon so why don't we go see about getting a tire for your car. And, Sweetie, your mother and I will see that you have enough to keep you from starving until you get settled," he grinned as he took her by the hand and they headed out to the tire store.

C.J. sat at his desk and realized how lucky he is to have a very dedicated and also competent staff to handle the everyday business of the resort because right now he can't get his thoughts off of Jessica and how much he wants her to come to the beach. *I don't quite understand all this protectiveness I feel toward her, but it has been great to have her to hold, kiss, and care about like I did Peggy. Actually, it almost seems like I'm more conscience of Jessica's needs than I was of Peggy's. Maybe that has faded over the years, too, but I really don't remember being so wrapped up in Peggy's life.*

But then, all of a sudden, a vision that wouldn't go away was showing him that Jessica wasn't coming because she realized she wouldn't have a job at the church until next year. "No," he yelled as he slammed the mail he had just picked up back down on his desk. "She can't decide not to come." He picked up the intercom and asked Emily if she could please come in.

"What's up, Boss?" she asked when she'd come in and shut the door. The look on his face had told her that he was upset about something.

"I just had an awful feeling that Jessica isn't coming because she doesn't have a job to come to. We both know she won't accept charity, so what are we going to do about it?"

"Well, C.J., I hadn't given too much thought to that part of her coming. I thought you had that all figured out. You had mentioned starting a pre-school in the hotel, but I'm not sure we have room or even if it would be a good decision."

"I had meant to look around to see if there might be a small building we could rent by the month, but it completely slipped my mind with the graduation and everything. Do you happen to know of any building that might be vacant?"

"There's that small building, just down the street, that's stood empty now for quite a while, but I don't know what condition it would be in or why it's not rented. If we could get it, we'd have all summer to clean it up and get it ready. Do you want me to check it out?"

"No, Kiddo, you came through again with the information I need, and I could kiss you for it. I don't know why I didn't think about that building. It would make a perfect little pre-school, and besides, I know the owner. I'll get right on it. I knew I had to be doing something right when I got you to come to work for me." He came around his desk and gave her a big hug and a kiss on the forehead.

"Now, C, J., was a kiss on the forehead all that information was worth?" she giggled.

"No, Ma'am." He quickly proceeded to pull her to her feet and then gave her a very nice affectionate kiss, which had her knees going a little weak.

"Oh, C.J., if you've kissed Jessica like that, she should be on her way very soon to get some more of those," she gasped. "I really need to find me a man," she mumbled.

"Oh, I gave Jessica one with a lot more feeling than that one, Em, but I hope you're right about her coming to get some more real soon. I'm ready and willing to oblige her, and I hope you can find a man worthy of you."

Jessica and her dad had taken both cars as they were going to leave hers at the shop to get a good tune-up along with the new tire. Gary North, the head mechanic and part owner, had dated Jill when they were in high school, and they knew he would check the car over thoroughly for any problems. He's married now to a real sweet girl he met while he was attending the Automotive Maintenance School, and they have a little boy a little over a year old. He told them he would deliver it sometime tomorrow when it was finished.

Her dad dropped her off at home as he had to go to the office to do some paper work, so she went back to her sorting. She decided to clean out her purse and maybe even change purses since it is now June and calling for summer accessories. As she was doing that, she pulled out a paper and realized it was the program from the concert last Sunday night. "What a wonderful night that was," she softly told herself, and she began recalling all the events of the evening. Of course, she couldn't forget that extraordinary, exceptional, emotional, and affectionate kiss C.J. had given her in the car. She lay back across the bed as her thoughts continued. *"Oh, C.J., I wish you were here or I was there so you could give me another one of those kisses."* And then, all of a sudden, the realization hit her. *"I really and truly love him, and I have to be on my way as soon as possible."* She tried to imagine a kiss from C.J. but decided nothing but the real thing would do. Her packing became more in earnest now because she knows she has to see C.J. very, very soon. Gary had said he would have her car back tomorrow, which is Friday, so she would spend a nice weekend with her family and then be on her way Monday morning. She was so excited that she had to call C.J. and let him know that she was coming. She could hardly wait for the phone to be answered.

C.J. had taken off shortly after his talk with Emily, and he was coming back in the door when the phone started ringing. Emily was just picking up the receiver when she noticed that he was smiling, and he'd motioned for her to come to his office. He was almost to his office door when Emily let out a squeal and he turned to see what that was all about. Emily was grinning and jumping and then he heard her say, "Yes, Honey, he's here. I'll put him right on." She immediately got very serious as she said, "Mr. C.J. Peterson, there's a Jessica Hale on the phone who would like to speak to you."

His heart was thumping like Thumper's foot when he lifted the receiver and tried to act businesslike when he said, "C.J. Peterson here, may I help you?"

"C.J., this is Jessica, are you busy with someone? I can call back or you can call me at a more convenient time."

"No, Jess, this is fine. Emily was acting so serious when she told me a Jessica Hale was on the phone that I decided to continue the businesslike manner. It's so good to hear from you. Did you call about something special or just to hear my lonely voice?"

"Could it be a little of both?" she giggled. "I can't believe it's only been three days since you left here, but this afternoon while I was packing clothes and getting together the other things I want to bring, I ran across the program from the concert. I tried to relive the kiss you gave me in the car but realized nothing but the real thing will do, and I'd like very much to experience that again as soon as possible.

My car is at the shop being checked and the new

tire put on, and it'll be all done by tomorrow. I've decided to spend the weekend with my family, and then I'm going to be on my way Monday morning by at least 10 o'clock. That is, if you still want me to come."

"Of course, I want you to come. Why would you think otherwise? In fact, I have an idea that I think you'll like, but I'm going to wait and show you rather than try to tell you about it. Does that make you curious enough to get here as soon as you can?"

"Oh, C.J., you can't do that to me. You have to tell me something about this new idea of yours. Please?"

"Sorry, Miss Hale, but there is nothing more I can say at this time, and I have to go now because I have someone here who needs to talk to me. I look forward to seeing you on Monday. Goodbye for now." He hung up on her and was immediately sorry.

CHAPTER SIXTEEN

W hew!" he said with a smile as he saw Emily peeking in the door to see if he was off the phone, and he motioned for her to come in. "I used the excuse 'someone's at the door' to end the conversation because I knew she would beg and I couldn't have refused her, but I would love for it to be a big surprise when she gets here."

"Refused her what, C.J.? You had a big smile on that face of yours when you came in the door. Does that mean you had some luck?"

"Big time, Em, but I really wanted to wait until I could take her to the building and she could see it in person. I'm about to call her back, though, because I don't want her to be upset with me. She may still change her mind and not come."

"She'll be here Monday!" Emily exclaimed as she shut the door and settled into one of the comfortable chairs. "I'm so excited and you have to be, too, but what's the scoop on this building?"

"I'll get to that, but I'm a little concerned about how I talked to Jess. I just told her I had an idea I thought she would like, but I was going to wait and show her instead of using the phone. I cut short our conversation so she couldn't coax me into telling her."

"You may have her here a lot sooner by pulling a trick like that," she laughed, "but please tell me what the dope is on the building before I go crazy. I think I can understand a little of what Jessica is going through, and maybe you should call her back."

"Well, the owner was really excited about the possibility of a pre-school being there. He said he's had several inquiries about buying or renting the building, but he'd always hoped to get something worthwhile in there so had been waiting for the right person to come along. He says he doesn't really need the money and he'll give us the summer, rent free, if we'll do the inside decorating. He will see that the fenced-in back yard is cleaned and secure, and he will even donate a couple outdoor activity centers."

"Did you get to see the inside so you'd know how much redecorating we would have to do?"

"It used to be a small veterinarian grooming and dog-sitting service until they outgrew it and moved to a larger building. It has two smaller rooms and the rest rooms on one side of the building, and there's a door leading to the play area on the back. The large room held a receptionist's desk, which is still there, by the way, and the reception room for the clients to wait with their pets, but the whole building has a good vinyl tile floor so it can be cleaned and sanitized easily. The place is in very good shape except for some paint and elbow grease to spruce it up. The entrance steps in front and back are wide with short risers and only two of them, but I thought if maneuvering steps was one of the things the little ones need to practice, these would be good for that, too. So, what do you think, Partner?"

"What do you mean, Partner? It sounds to me like you struck gold, Mr. Peterson. I'm so excited and I'm pretty good with a paint brush. I'll be ready to work whenever the one in charge gives the order. I'm curious, though, who this mysterious owner is that you said you knew. Should I know him, too?"

"I think you've met him, Em. I met him when we closed the deal on the resort because he was helping the owner with the sale. I have taken him out on the boat several times, but he has always said he'd meet me at the marina. His name is Mel Jackson, but he likes to be called Jackson."

"Jackson owns that building? I've definitely met him, C.J.--we've taken him to the band concert at the High School, Silly. He's such a sweet guy, and he used to be a teacher, right?"

"Yes he was, and that's probably why he's thrilled to have the building become a small pre-school. But, do you think I should call Jess back and give a little hint of what I've found, or should I make her wait?"

"That's a hard one, C.J., because both have merit. I'd love to see her face when she sees what you've found, but I can also understand what she is going through. She may not be able to enjoy the weekend with her family." Just then the phone started ringing and C.J. picked it up so Emily wouldn't have to run to the desk. "Beachside, may I help you?"

"C.J., is that you?" Jessica's shy soft voice came through the line.

"Yes, Jess, it's me. Am I going to get the third degree for cutting our conversation a little short before?"

"Oh, no, not anything like that. I was just wondering if you could give me a little hint about your idea so I can try to relax over the weekend with my family. I've been so excited since our talk, and I'm not sure I'll be able to keep my thoughts on my driving Monday if I don't have a little information on what you want to show me. Please, C.J., tell me just a little something, anything, to satisfy my curiosity until I get there. Pretty, pretty please?"

"I knew she could do this," he whispered to Em as he covered the mouthpiece.

"You can't leave her up in the air for four days, C.J., so tell her something. Good luck," Em also whispered as she backed out of his office.

"Jess...Honey...it's not going to be as exciting to hear about it on the phone as it would be to see it, but I can understand how you're feeling, so here goes. Em and I were talking about you not having a job when you get here, and I was afraid that you might change your mind and not come. So, with

Em's help, I have found a small building which is rent free for the rest of the summer if we'll do some painting and cleaning up inside. It has one large room and two smaller ones, as well as two rest rooms inside, and a fenced-in play yard in the back that the owner says he will have cleaned up and made completely secure. It used to be a small veterinarian grooming and sitting service. There is a desk that I thought we could put in one of the smaller rooms for an office, and maybe the other could be used for storage and supplies. The floor is covered with a vinyl tile which can be cleaned and sanitized easily. Will that hold you until you get here Monday?"

"Oh, C.J., what can I say? You are the most wonderful person I've ever met, and I may have to start earlier Monday morning than I had planned," she giggled. "I can hardly wait to get that kiss I've been dreaming about all afternoon, and now I have a building to look at, too. What have I done to deserve all this?"

"Just being the wonderful person you are, Jess. You believe that God is in control of your life and you live accordingly."

"Well, I have a lot of supplies and ideas accumulated from the student teaching I did, and I've done a lot of painting so that's no problem. I'm just so excited, C.J., but I want you to know I love you for who you are and not just for what you've done and are doing for me."

"Thank you, Sweetie, and I'm impatiently waiting to give you that kiss you've been dreaming about, and for you to show me just how much you love me—by returning that kiss." Even though he'd had to chuckle when he'd heard her little gasp of surprise, he'd also quickly realized how she could've taken that remark. That's why he'd quickly added the extra words.

"Thank you so much for not making me wait for this wonderful news, C.J. I know Mom and Dad will be thrilled as will Jill and Jodi. Dad told me yesterday that they would be able to help me until I get settled so I can pay for a room, food, and get some publicity out about the opening of the school, like registration times and prices. There's a lot to do before the middle of August."

"Well, it sounds like your mind is running like a well-tuned school teacher so I'll let you go for now. Will you have your cell phone Monday so you can let me know where you are occasionally and how you're doing?"

"Yes, worrywart, I'll keep you posted."

"Where did that name come from? Is it a new creation of your generation or from a much older one?"

"I forgot that you weren't in my generation, Old Guy, but that word is one that my dad uses quite often to tease Mom. He thinks she worries too much. I'll probably call you or you can call me over the weekend, but whatever, I'll call you when I'm ready to leave on Monday so you can count the hours, minutes, and seconds. Bye now," she giggled.

"Bye, yourself, you Sassy Little Girl." Chuckling, he put the receiver down, and then just shook his head. *How could I have been so lucky that God would send me this bundle of excitement, energy, and innocence to care for and love? How can I still be holding back on committing fully to her? I definitely want to help her, protect her, hug and kiss her, but I do those things for Em, too. Well, the hugging and kissing with Em doesn't have the same effect on me as with Jess, but I'm just so afraid of losing again, like I did with Peggy. I guess I'll just have to take one day at a time and see what happens.*

Jessica couldn't keep the smile off her face or the gleam out of her eyes when all the family got home from work. They took one look at her and just sat down to hear the news they knew she was dying to tell them. When she finished, however, they were as excited as she was, and her dad, as was his custom, bowed his head to pray.

"Our Dear Heavenly Father, in your infinite love and mercy, you have again shown this family how you care for your children who put their trust and their hope in You. We are so grateful for this opportunity that has been given to Jessica, and we pray that the children she teaches will see your love in her words and actions. Everything seems to be happening so quickly for us, as humans, and it is hard to fully comprehend. However, we accept your plan and your timing and just ask that you continue to walk by Jessica's side, or even carry her, if need be, as she ventures into this new phase of her life. We ask your blessing on all of our family, including the new one who will be arriving in December, and we extend our asking to also include C.J. and T.J. and their parents, Brian and Jeannette. In your name we pray, Amen."

On Saturday, her mom and sisters were all trying to help her separate what she should take and what she wouldn't need. She was about ready to scream when she finally threw up her hands and said, "That's enough, already. I have just decided that I'm going to take only the bare necessities, like on a vacation, until I know for sure where I'm going to be living and have a place to put all the stuff you think I'm going to need. For all I know, I may be living out of my car for a few days, and then what would I do with all this? After all, I'm not going to be that far away, so I can come back and get things as I need them. I don't think you're planning to rent my room out for a little while, are you?" She'd smiled, but the tension in her voice had warned them to back off.

C.J. called Saturday evening but there was no answer. He got a little concerned, but she'd said she was going to spend a nice weekend with her family. *Just don't go getting too possessive, C.J. Remember what it did to Todd.* He left a message that he had called and hoped she was enjoying the weekend.

He was getting ready for bed when his cell phone rang. He almost panicked as he remembered the call he had received the night they had taken Peggy to the hospital. Her mother had called to tell him she had been diagnosed with meningitis. He'd rushed to be by her side, but could only watch as she slowly slipped away from him. He reached for the phone but could hardly say Hello.

"C.J., are you all right? Your voice sounds a little funny," he heard Jess's sweet voice and his heart returned to normal beating. "I hope it's not too late to call, but I got your message and wanted to tell you about our evening. All seven of us went out for a very nice dinner and then to a movie. We really had a great time except that you weren't with us." She was giggling as she was sure he was trying to figure out who the extra one was. "Don't you want to know who the seventh one was?" she asked.

"Well, I don't think the baby could've been born yet, so only if you want to tell me," he replied as nonchalantly as he could muster. "Just don't tell me Todd escaped from the hospital and came visiting again."

"Oh, C.J., I'm sorry. I didn't mean to upset you. I told you it was great except that you weren't with us. The seventh one tonight happened to be T.J. He called Jill last night and offered to drive down and take us all out for the evening. Wasn't that really nice of him?"

So my brother really has taken a step back into the real world. He realized Jess didn't know the story of T.J. and his broken heart, though, and it was too long a story for tonight so he replied, "My brother is getting to be quite the Romeo, I see. Do you think I should take some lessons from him so you'll be equally impressed with me when you get here?"

"Ah...I hardly know how to answer that, C.J. Do... do you think I was criticizing your conduct just because I said it had been nice of T.J. to drive down here and take us out?...I'm sorry if I haven't been expressing my thanks sufficiently enough for your satisfaction, but I..I could never be disappointed in what you've done for me an...and my family."

C.J. could tell that he had hurt her deeply because he could hear the catch in her voice as she was trying to hold back the tears. "Jess," he whispered softly, "please forgive me. I didn't mean it that way at all. When the phone rang, it brought back some memories that still haunt me at times, but I shouldn't have made that remark. I'd like to share some things with you sometime soon, but right now I hope you'll accept my apology."

Realizing how the phone call had reminded him of the night he'd been informed that Peggy had meningitis, she was immediately wishing she were there for him, but he didn't know that she even knew of Peggy. How was she going to comfort him? She decided to get off the subject all together. "Well, Mr. Peterson, I'll accept your apology and I'm looking forward to seeing you Monday and receiving that kiss we've mentioned, but I imagine it's getting about time to call it a day. What do you think?"

"I think you're right, Jess. Thank you for calling and I'll be waiting Monday with my lips puckered and ready."

"You're so funny, but I'm glad you want to satisfy my longings. Goodnight now."

"Goodnight, Jess. I'm really glad you had a good time tonight."

CHAPTER SEVENTEEN

True to her promise, Jessica called Monday morning to let C.J. and Em know that she was on her way. She had already reached the junction outside of Sanford and was now headed cross country on Rt. 421 to Dunn. Most of the fields had been planted and the foliage was green and lush along the road. She was so happy and singing along with music on the radio station which was playing mostly Christian music. The beginning verses of Psalm 46 came to her which says: 'God is our refuge and strength, an ever present help in trouble. Therefore, we will not fear, though the earth gives way and the mountains fall into the heart of the sea.'

"Well, I hope that doesn't happen for a long time," she murmured as she continued to listen to the radio which was now playing one of her favorite hymns. She smiled as she remembered that her dad had said something similar just the other day to one of the phrases of the song, something about God taking care of the things she was worrying about.

She had gotten to Dunn and was now taking a short ride on Rt. 55 over to Rt. I-40 which would take her to Wrightsville Beach. Then it would be just a short jaunt up to Big Breaker. Since she'd left home a little before 9 o'clock, she now whispered, "If I'm lucky, I can be there for lunch."

I-40 wasn't heavy with traffic so she was making good time until she saw flashing lights ahead and her spirits spiraled downward as she could imagine a long wait because of an accident. She was elated, however, when it was only a five minute delay but so sorry to see that a deer had been hit. The car had received considerable damage to the grill and the windshield, and an ambulance was there to apparently take someone to the hospital. She whispered a short prayer for the injured and also for her safety on the rest of the trip. When she reached the junction to Wrightsville Beach, her heart started pounding like crazy as she knew she was only about 20 minutes away from C.J. and the kiss she'd been dreaming of.

She suddenly heard a siren and saw flashing lights coming up behind her at a high rate of speed. She quickly pulled to the side of the road as she thought her foot must've gotten a little heavy on the gas pedal in her rush to get to her destination. *Why couldn't I keep my mind on what I was doing?*

She sat in puzzlement as the squad car zipped by

her and was way up the road in just seconds. "Thank you, Dear Jesus," she murmured. "You are certainly keeping your promises today; and now, let's see if I can keep my mind on my driving and get to Big Breaker Beach all in one piece."

When she pulled into the parking area at Beachside Resort, she was so relieved that she dropped her head on the steering wheel to relax just a minute, but, apparently she'd hit the horn and it started beeping and wouldn't stop. She was so embarrassed but she got that taken care of just as C.J. and Emily reached her door, laughing and yelling, "Open Up or we'll break the door down."

She then realized the doors were still locked because she hadn't turned the engine off or put it in Park. She tried to cover her face with one hand and shook her head negatively while she did the shifting, reached for the key, and unlocked the door with the other. C.J. opened the door, reached in and gave her a wonderful welcoming hug, unbuckled the seat belt and then said, "You must've had quite a morning, Jess, to be that anxious to let us know you'd arrived, or do you always make an appearance like that?" He chuckled as he extended his hand to help her out, but she didn't move and then he saw the tears in her eyes quickly overflowing and running down her cheeks.

"Jess, what's wrong?" he asked as his arms went around her and pulled her close to his chest.

"Everything," she sobbed. "First there was an accident, a deer was hit and someone was hurt, apparently, because the ambulance was there. Then I thought I was going to get a ticket just this side of Wrightsville Beach. A squad car that had been a ways behind me for a mile or so suddenly turned on his siren and flashing lights, and was almost up to me by the time I slowed down and pulled over, but then he went flying on by. I guess I should've known he wasn't going to stop when he was going so fast, but then to top off the whole trip, the dumb horn had to get stuck when I was just going to relax a minute before coming in. Could anything get any worse?"

"Oh, yes, a lot worse. You could have been in the accident, you could have gotten a ticket, and you could have not gotten here. I think you were very lucky, Miss Hale, like maybe someone was watching over you and answering a lot of prayers. Isn't that the way you should look at it?"

She sheepishly grinned, "You sound just like my father—always the optimist."

"I've realized lately that's the way to look at life— roll with the punches believing that God will be there when you're in trouble and also when you're very happy, as I am now that you're here safe and sound. And you made it in time for lunch because Em and I were just getting ready to go eat. Come and join us, Sweetie. Jackie is sitting with a little baby all day today so she can't join us. She was really happy to hear that you were coming back, though."

"I was hoping I would get here in time to eat with you, but I was beginning to doubt I'd make it when that squad car appeared," she grinned as she finally took his hand that he'd offered and let him help her out of the car. She went into Emily's arms for a hug and then the three of them, arm in arm, headed for the deli.

By the time lunch was finished, C.J. was overly anxious to show her the building he'd found, but when Jessica actually saw it, he thought her beautiful eyes were shining like diamonds. She'd immediately started to talk about what colors of paint she would need to buy, and maybe she could afford enough lumber to divide the two colors she wanted to make the walls of the school room. The room sizes also pleased her, and the outdoor play yard was just perfect. She turned to look at him, saw that cute grin and asked, "C.J., are you sure we can have this rent free for the summer if we do the inside decorating?"

"That's what the owner told me," he said and then seemed to be ready when he realized she was standing on tip-toe as she threw her arms around his neck. He picked her up so he could swing her around and then held her at the exact height so they could kiss without her stretching.

"Have you grown since you left last Tuesday?" she giggled.

"I don't think we've ever kissed standing up before, but I like it. Is this where you want to receive the kiss you've been waiting for since the night of the concert? That first one was just a warm-up kiss before the real thing, right?" He was laughing as he lifted her up again and gave her a long affectionate kiss which had her feeling tingles she'd never felt before. "I think we'll wait for a cleaner spot to relive the one in T.J.'s car. Do you want to check out anything more before we go back to the Beachside?"

"I'd like to take a look in the two smaller rooms and check the rest rooms if you don't mind." So, returning to the inspection of the building, they discovered some chairs in the closets of the small rooms, and they were unique because they were in sets of three that were fastened on a frame that could be raised or lowered. They had probably been used in the reception room of the Grooming and Sitting Service. There were four sets which would give her just the number of seats she would need for the twelve students she had already determined she could handle in each class of each age group. Two classes of four year olds could attend on Monday, Wednesday, and Friday, and two classes of three year olds would come on Tuesdays and Thursdays. "Little ones like bright colors," she said aloud although in deep thought, and then C.J. saw that gleam in her eyes that made him sure she had made at least one decision.

The three of them went to Emily's for a home-cooked meal, and they all pitched in to help prepare it. The conversation didn't vary far from the plans Jessica had for the next few days, but C.J. did get to ask a little more about the night her family spent with T.J. Of course, Emily got to talk about the architect who was staying at the Resort and working on the addition to the church, but finally they decided to have some hot tea before C.J. left, hoping it would relax them so they could all sleep well. Of course, Jessica had called her folks to tell them all about the building and her trip before falling into bed.

Whether it was the tea or the exhaustion of the trip and the excitement of seeing the building, Jessica slept well and was then up ready to tackle the job she saw ahead of her. She'd decided the first thing she needed to do was go to the store for a broom, a dust pan, window cleaner, tile floor cleaner, a mop, paper towels, etc. The spider webs and dust have to get out of there first before she can begin to paint. The lumber yard would be next so she could get the 1x4's that would serve as the divider between the colors, but she'd have to do some measuring before she could do that. She was also thinking she could put wooden pegs or hooks along the divider for backpacks and light jackets. *It will call for a good carpenter for that job so everything won't look like it's going downhill. Oh, I wonder if the owner will object to that because it will surely put nail holes along the walls. I'd better have C.J. check before I do anything other than clean right now. That will keep me busy for a couple of days, at least. I could always paint first and then decide whether to use the wood or a wallpaper border to accent the change of colors. That sounds like a good idea, so I think I'll plan that way. I'll get a carpenter to come and give me a straight line to paint by, and then we'll decide where to go from there. I'll talk to the guys at the lumber yard and get their advice, or maybe I should talk to C.J. Do you suppose he might be handy with a yardstick and level?*

Emily had begged Jessica to stay with her for the summer, at least, because now that she had her own car, she could come and go as she wished. She also promised to help each day, when she was through at the resort so the work should go fairly fast.

One morning, Jessica went to the church and talked to the pastor about their plans for a kindergarten. She met his wife, who was going to be one of the teachers, at least until they could find others to fill the positions. " A pastor's wife can be a full time job without a job of teaching," she'd grinned. They were thrilled to meet Jessica and learn about the small school she'd be opening this fall. A position would definitely be held for her in their planning in case her endeavor didn't work out.

The reality of the whole situation hit Jessica one afternoon as she started a list of the other items that would be needed to make a pre-school operative, and just how many little students she would need to be able to pay the rent, buy supplies, and have something left to pay for her own needs. Now she knew why most pre-schools were in churches, homes that had no mortgage, or schools supported by the State. She sat on the floor in the middle of the room, wrapped her arms around her drawn-up knees, and cried.

She hadn't realized it was after 4 o'clock until she heard the door open and Emily and C.J. came bouncing in. She took one look at their happy faces and sobbed all the harder. They were immediately on the floor beside her, thinking she may have gotten hurt, and C.J. had her in his arms asking, "What's the problem, Jess? Are you hurt or what?"

"W-we ca-can't da-do this," she muttered as she tried not to cry but to no avail. She knew she sounded like a juvenile, but she couldn't help it. C.J. continued to hold her and stroke her hair.

"Can you tell Em and me what this is all about?" he asked after a couple minutes of hugging her and shrugging his shoulders at Em.

"I was doing some calculating this afternoon and making a list of the items that still would be needed before I could open a pre-school, and I ju-just ca-can't af-ford it, af-after all the wu-work you ha-have hel-helped me da-do," her sobs now turning to hiccups.

"We're not going to talk another minute about the cost to get this pre-school open and operating. The owner of the building and I both knew approximately what the cost was going to be and worked it out. I thought you would be too involved with all this," as he gestured around the room, "to be worrying about expenses. How wrong I was again, Jess, for not realizing how thoroughly independent you are and what I still need to learn about you. I'll talk to you about the finances later, but right now, don't we have some more work to do?"

When she mentioned having a carpenter come to draw the lines to paint by, and her concern about the nail holes, C.J. said, "Drawing the lines is taken care of, and I'll talk to Jackson about the wooden divider along the wall." When she mentioned the tables that would be needed, he smiled and said, "That's all taken care of, too."

He went out to his car and returned with a yardstick, a level, and a marking pencil. As he set to work, he looked at her puzzled face and smiled as he remarked, "There's also a lot you need to learn about me, Sweetheart. I haven't just been sitting at my desk the last five years. I took some woodworking classes in high school, and it's amazing how some things you learn in those insignificant workshops can help when you really start living."

"I wonder if what I learned in my Home Economics classes will ever help me with my cooking and sewing when I really start living," she giggled.

"Are you saying you can't cook, Miss Hale? I may have to do some reconsidering about you. I had you all figured out as the All American Girl who could do anything she set her mind to."

"I didn't say I couldn't cook, Mr. Peterson. I only remarked that the things I learned in my classes may never help me in the kitchen or at the sewing machine. You shouldn't be so quick to jump to conclusions," she smirked, but a mischievous smile came through her eyes loud and clear.

"Yes, Ma'am, I'll try to remember that," he chuckled.

CHAPTER EIGHTEEN

On Friday, C.J. knew that Emily had a dinner date again with Kevin, the architect, so he decided to ask Jessica if she would please stop working early and let him take her on a date. He felt she needed some time away from just cleaning, painting, and planning.

So, when he dropped in to see her about 10 o'clock, he took her in his arms and got her attention. "It has been four days since you arrived here on Monday, Jess, and not once have you stopped for any relaxation. Therefore, I want you to quit working early today so I can take you on a real date tonight, and I thought we might drive into Wilmington."

Jessica reluctantly agreed to his 'order' about quitting early today and the date, but she also knew that she'd been pushing all of them pretty hard and they needed a rest. "You win, Mr. Peterson. When I get to a stopping place sometime this afternoon, I'll quit and take the whole weekend off, if that will make you happy," she rather disgustedly remarked and then grinned at him as she poured more paint into the tray.

She was busy painting the small room toward the front of the building that she had chosen for her office. She'd selected the dark green she'd also picked for the lower 3 feet of the school room. She thought the darker color would help keep scuffs from showing that are almost inevitable when children are playing. The upper portion of that room will be a creamy yellow for brightness, and she'd found some roller shades for the windows that have cartoon characters on them. She explained to C.J. that she would pull the shades for rest time and during story time.

"It definitely saves my voice," she remarked, "because the students quickly learn that when the shades come down, it's time for them to find their places and get quiet." The creamy yellow paint will also be used in the other small room as she felt the lighter color would make it easier to locate the items she planned to store in there.

With the three of them having worked at least part of each day this week, they had cleaned out all the accumulation of dirt and wiped down the walls so they are all ready for painting. They'd also cleaned the windows inside and out (of course, C.J. got to do the outside), scrubbed the floors and the restrooms. They realized the windows and floors will need some more cleaning, after the painting is done, but they wanted them clean to begin with so no dirt would get into their brushes and rollers.

Jessica had worked on the desk and had it shining like new, and so today, she had started painting the first room. To break the dark green of the walls in her office, she'd first painted the ceiling white and would also paint the woodwork around the doors and the two windows white. A finishing touch will be to hang some white-framed pictures on the walls.

The rest rooms would both have the white walls with the dark green ceilings, so they'd look just a little lower, and the vanity cabinets, which are a little old and in need of some TLC, would be sanded and painted the dark green, too. A wallpaper border will be installed at the cabinet height and pictures or wooden cut-outs will decorate the walls to break the stark white. She might paper the walls below the border although that would be harder to clean.

"Getting back to your taking the whole weekend off, Miss Hale, are you really and truly serious?" he asked as he looked rather skeptically at her. "Jess, if you'll do that, I'll plan to take you out on the boat so you can really relax sometime over the weekend."

"I'll definitely do that if I get to go on the boat," she quickly promised. "I've been dreaming of doing that again ever since I went back to school after Spring break."

"Okay, you've got a deal, Cutie. I'd better get back, but I'll see you at lunch time. I'll bring something over here and we can sit outside while we eat. It really looks great out back since they got it all cleaned up. I understand Jackson is going to refinish or maybe even replace the fence before he's through. See you later."

"I guess I'm going to eat outside for lunch," she giggled as she watched him exit the building and jog toward the hotel. He seemed to do it so effortlessly and her heart was, of course, pounding as she offered a short prayer. "Dear Jesus, I don't know what I have ever done to deserve C.J. in my life, or the opportunity to open this pre-school and help little ones before they start Kindergarten, but I thank You with all my heart. I intend to do my best to be a good example to the children and to their parents. With your help, I know I'll be able to succeed."

With the ceiling already painted, she got busy and had two walls finished and the third one well started by the time C.J. came with sandwiches, a juicy peach which had been peeled and sliced, and iced tea. It was delicious, and the weather was beautiful as they sat on the back steps.

"Jess, would you rather go on the boat this evening than drive into Wilmington? I had thought we might ask Emily and Kevin to join us tomorrow or Sunday afternoon on the boat, but if you want to go tonight, it's all right with me."

When she didn't answer right away, he glanced over at her but couldn't read her expression at all. Putting his arm across her shoulders, he pulled her toward him and kissed her on the forehead. "What are you thinking, Sweetie?"

"Ah...I...I don't know how to say what I'm feeling, C.J., and ah...I'm afraid you'll think I'm a very ungrateful or selfish person, but I don't mean it to be that way. Ah...my mind is going one direction, but my heart is going another. How can I say I want to go on the boat tonight with just the two of us without sounding selfish? It's just that it has been the three of us together all week and I feel like I want you to myself for awhile. I do sound selfish, don't I?" She put her face in her hands and groaned.

C.J. couldn't keep from laughing as he watched her. "Oh, Jess, if I could only lock you up and keep you just the way you are today, I'd be the happiest guy alive. Of course, I'd want to take you out of the locked up place whenever I wanted some of your charm, and that would be constantly." He reached over and turned her face toward him, wiped a smug of paint off her cheek and then tilted her face so he could give her a long meaningful kiss. "I'm so very, very intrigued by you, Jess," he chuckled, "and you may definitely have your wish. I would much rather be on the boat than driving to Wilmington on a Friday night. If we plan to go about 6 o'clock, will that give you enough time? We'll either eat on the boat or sail down to one of the good restaurants along the coast."

"Yes, I'll be ready by 6, but would you mind if I wanted to eat on the boat, too?"

"Not at all, Sweetheart, I prefer to have *you* all to myself, too." Still chuckling, he got up and pulled her up from the steps. "You'd better get moving if you're going to finish your office today. I'll run along and make preparations for a relaxing evening for just the two of us," he grinned as he opened the door, gave her a little helpful push, and then he was gone.

It was now 4:30 but she was so satisfied with the room. She had not only finished the walls, but had gotten the woodwork painted, too. "One room completed," she sighed as she took one last glance before leaving.

Luckily, Em was out of the shower when she got there, so Jess was able to shower and let Em back in to work on her hair and make-up. Fastening her wavy hair back into a pony tail, she pulled on a pair of crop pants and a tank top and grabbed a long-sleeved shirt to put on if it cooled down or the bugs got too bad. She had just gotten out the door and was headed to her car to drive to the Beachside when she saw C.J. pulling up. He quickly got out of his car; and as he came toward her, he said, "This is a date, Jessica Hale, and on my dates, I come and pick up my girl. Now get back in the house so I can do this right."

She wasn't sure whether to take him seriously or not, but as he headed straight for the front door, she scampered back inside the house just as he rang the bell. "Hi, Jess," he greeted her and gave her that captivating grin. "Are you ready for an evening on the water? It's a lovely night and you look sweet and fresh enough to eat without a speck of paint anywhere," he chuckled.

She heard Em in the living room so called to her, "Come here a minute, Em, I need to ask you something." When Em appeared in the foyer, Jess asked, "Is this really the C.J. that we know and have been working with all week? This one is acting a little strange."

They all laughed as he opened the screen door and grabbed her hand. "Get out here, you little smart aleck, and let's get on our way." Looking back at Em, he said, "Have a nice time tonight, but be sure to remember our motto. "Don't do anything I wouldn't do!"

"Aw shucks," she laughed.

It was absolutely delightful on the water and C.J. set the sails and let the wind do its thing. They sat on the seat across the stern and ate the fabulous meal he'd had the chef prepare for them. Delicious club sandwiches, chips, celery sticks, and iced tea would have been enough, but Jess was completely surprised when he brought out the dessert. It was a bunch of yummy chocolate dipped strawberries that were so juicy and delicious. What a great way to finish their meal and to make sure they were stuffed.

There were questions that Jess wanted to ask, but she wasn't sure if this was the right time. Finally, she decided to jump in with both feet. "C.J., please tell me if you don't want to talk about your past, but you've mentioned just enough to make me a bit curious. You pretty well know my experience with Todd, and I would like to know what you've been through. You were quite adamant that first day about how you felt when so many girls were chasing you, so I was wondering if you have a reason why you feel that way."

"I've been trying to find the right time to tell you about my past, Jess, and I guess this is as good a time as any. At the beginning of my junior year of high school, I started dating Peggy, and we both soon felt we were the perfect match. After graduation, I tried to talk her into going to UNC so we could be together, but she had her heart set on Vassar. It was working out all right as we'd had our summers together, kept in touch almost daily by phone and e-mail, and she came home quite often on weekends. The years seem to pass fairly fast and we were in our junior year of college when one night, maybe a little past midnight, the phone rang. It was her mother calling to tell me they had been called to the college because Peggy had taken ill.

By the time they'd arrived, she was extremely feverish and incoherent so they'd called the ambulance that took her to the hospital. She was put through several tests, diagnosed with meningitis, and was in critical condition. I rushed to the hospital only to find her in quarantine and I could only see her through the window and plastic covering. I stood there the rest of the night, watching as she kept slipping further away, and then she was gone. I really don't know how I finished that year of school or the next. I wanted my life to be over so I could join her, wherever she was. I think my parents were very afraid that I'd try to commit suicide, and I may have if it hadn't been for T.J. who kept telling me it would get better for me as it had for him.

You see, T.J. had a heartbreaking experience, also, and I kept watching and waiting for him to lose control so we could end our lives together. He never did, although he'd never date a girl over once or twice, and when he started his practice with Dad, about three years ago, he stopped dating altogether.

He and Adele had met and dated for a couple of years during his Pre-Med and then he gave her a diamond for Christmas during his first year of Med School. They planned to be married the next year in June. He didn't believe in sex before marriage as we both had been taught it was best to wait, and we had both accepted that was the way to go. So, when Adele tried to lure him into sleeping with her in April, he told her he guessed they could get married a little sooner if she was getting so impatient. However, he'd also informed her that he'd still prefer to wait until June, as they had planned, because his classes were too difficult to miss any days for taking a honeymoon or giving much attention to her.

She apparently went into a rage and finally told him she was carrying another man's child. She threw the ring at him, stormed out of his room, and literally disappeared. She wasn't from the Chapel Hill area and her parents refused to tell T.J. anything. They did accuse him of breaking his promises of abstinence and inferring that he was the one who was to blame for her pregnancy and then wouldn't marry her. We had to assume she had lied to her parents, but where she went, nobody knows. T.J. finally had to give up when his attempts to find her failed. After all, he had Med School, intern obligations, and residency years all still ahead of him.

So, when he showed quite an interest in Jill the night we had dinner at my parents, I was surprised but really thrilled because I thought maybe we two brothers could possibly turn the corner together. I know my life has changed since you came into it, Jess, and I am praying that this is God's leading. I have finally felt that perhaps I can love someone again fully and sincerely without worrying about another tragedy happening, but it is still hard to put the past behind me." He pulled her into his arms and kissed her so affectionately and with so much feeling, she felt she wanted to belong to him for life, but she also feared that emotions could easily get out of control here on the boat. She pulled away and stood to watch the sun setting like a big ball of fire.

"Jess," C.J. said in almost a whisper, "did these experiences that T.J. and I had to go through make you think less of us?"

"Oh, C.J., please don't ever think that," she said with tears in her eyes. "I'm so excited just to be with you, and I'm only afraid my emotions are out of control. Please let me have a few minutes to regain my composure."

"Of course," he said as he moved to check the sails. "This hasn't been the night I would have ordered," he said softly, "but you know the truth now and can still say you're excited to be with me. That's not so bad," he chuckled.

They sailed a little longer before he turned back toward the marina. They had been sharing some more of their past, mostly about growing up, and he'd told her that Em had a story, too, but it was up to her to decide when it was time to share it.

Jess only nodded as she understood how that would certainly be true. She was a little curious, though, and hoped it wouldn't be long before her friend would confide in her. Then they'd all know the hard times that seem to have touched each of their lives.

CHAPTER NINETEEN

While C.J. walked her to the door, he was saying, "I've had a wonderful time with you tonight, Jess, and we'll have to do it again real soon. It will be without the stories of the past next time though."

He smiled and then his lips met hers, and his embrace had their bodies tight and firm against each other. He was deepening the kiss and also moving his hands a little lower to pull her even closer, and Jessica knew he could feel her heart pumping way overtime, and she could feel the thumping in his chest, too. She tried to push away, but his hands were now securely locked around her hips. She started to panic and then she couldn't stop her trembling. He immediately dropped his arms to his side and took a step back. "I'm so sorry, Jess. I didn't mean to scare you, but maybe it's a good thing you gave me the signal to stop. I could get carried away so easily with you tonight, but I know that's not what either one of us wants. We'll talk about our future another time." With an "I'm sorry," and a peck on the cheek, he opened the door for her and then headed back to his car.

Emily came home about 30 minutes later, and the smile on her face revealed what kind of an evening she'd had with this new man in her life, Kevin Bradley. "He is such a nice gentleman, Jess, but I'm having a hard time putting my past behind me and realizing life can actually go on."

"C.J. told me about Peggy and also about Adele tonight, Em. It's hard to believe that those two wonderful brothers both had to face such tragedies."

"I'm so glad he told you himself, although I had let you in on some of it. Now, I guess, it's time for me to tell you *my* story. C.J. and I have referred to the three of us as The Three Musketeers of Tragedy, but we haven't told T.J. yet of the name. We may have to change it to The Four Musketeers since you joined our club, but I'm hoping and praying we may get to change it to the Four Happy Musketeers. Since you came into our lives, Jess, everything seems to be improving, and life is looking brighter for all of us. Let's get into bed and then I'll give you my tale of woe, unless you're too tired tonight."

"Of course not. I want to know all about what you had to face and how you're coping with it. If I have helped, it is only because God led me here, but I'll always feel that I was found by you two wonderful people for my rescue from a life of abuse and also for a great future."

They got settled in bed, with pillows stacked behind them so they could sit against them comfortably, and then Jess waited for Em to talk.

"I don't know exactly where to start," she began, "but I've mentioned that I grew up next door to the Petersons, and they were marvelous neighbors. We had cookouts, went on hikes and vacations together, took bike rides together, played games together, and besides all that, it included my first puppy love crush on T.J. He was a year older than I was and C.J. was two years younger. They both, of course, just considered me the tomboy from next door since I was an only child and had to play with the boys."

Jessica chuckled and said, "Now I understand why C.J. referred to you as a tomboy when we were talking in his office one day."

Em laughed, "I don't doubt it, but we finally grew up and T.J. went off to college. During his junior year he started bringing Adele home quite a bit since she was from out of state. This may overlap a little, since C.J. has told you about T.J., but the next two years were heartbreaking for me, as I watched my hero with that other girl. Of course, I was in college, a sophomore, and thankfully only saw them occasionally. I dated, but my heart always pounded whenever I saw T.J.

When Adele pulled her stunt, C.J. was a sophomore at UNC and had been dating Peggy for over three years. He had really been disappointed when she wouldn't go to UNC with him, but they worked it out.

After I had graduated with a degree in Business, Jeannette asked if I would like to work with her at the Antique Store. I was ecstatic because I had always loved going there with my folks and admiring the beautiful things they had displayed. Jeannette and I had become quite close, and when C.J. lost Peggy, we worried and mourned together.

I'd worked there about three years when, one day, a young, extremely handsome guy came into the store. He told Jeannette and me that he was moving to Chapel Hill as soon as his house was completed, and since he loved antiques and wanted to furnish his house with at least a few, he'd been told that this was the store that he should visit. We were excited, of course, and I was even more so when he asked me out a month later on one of his frequent 'fly-in business trips.' I'd noticed there was no ring on his finger, even though that doesn't mean anything these days, but it made me anxious to learn more about him.

We had dated for over a year, whenever he was in town on business, and then he asked me to marry him. He had driven me by a house he said he was building, which looked really nice from the street. Well, we planned a February wedding and everything was going along too perfectly, I guess, because three days before the wedding, he was arrested as a con artist. He'd apparently had several girls, scattered across the country, that he had conned out of all their savings to help get his business started in their town, but it turned out there was no business and he'd disappear as soon as he got the money. He had even talked to me about a loan, and my folks were just about ready to help their new son-in-law when the FBI swooped down on him. I was crushed and so humiliated, and I don't know what I would have done if C.J. hadn't come and asked if I would be willing to help him at the resort. Of course, I'd known about the purchase and Jeannette encouraged me, actually, so I could report to them on how C.J. was coping. It had been over three years, I think, since Peggy had died, and this opportunity to own a resort was the first sign they had seen of him wanting to live. It's been five long, but so exciting, workaholic years now, but as he probably told you, he had no interest in the girls who came here and made fools of themselves trying to get his attention. But, when he came into the lobby that day with you in his arms, I saw a look of excitement, of a passion, even, that I hadn't seen on his face for eight long years. He truly adores you, Jess, I just know it, and I'm praying that you both can find a lasting happiness together.

I've been somewhat like C.J., afraid to take a chance on another man, but Kevin has told me all about his past, his struggle to get his firm off the ground, and his goals for the future, and I feel very comfortable with him. However, I'm taking it mighty slow this time, and although I don't feel great about it, I've researched his firm on the Net and it is definitely legitimate. And now, you know all there is to know about Emily, C.J. and T.J."

"Just one thing I'm curious about that I haven't taken time to ask about. What does the C.J. and T.J. stand for?"

"I've been wondering how long it would take you to get to that," she laughed. "I've called them by their initials since we were little kids, so it's almost impossible for me to think they have other names. C.J. stands for Cameron James, T.J. stands for Terence James, and if you ever hear some of their father's friends or family talk to him, it would be B.J., not Brian. As I heard the story, James Peterson was Brian's grandfather, apparently an outstanding man and greatly admired by his family. Consequently, James has become the middle name of all the male descendants, starting with Brian's father, Malcolm James, who was an only child. Brian has two brothers, however, so all three have James as their middle name, and there are several cousins of C.J. and T.J. who also carry the name.

I think that's enough background stories for tonight, don't you? Unless, of course, there's a good story about your evening with the handsome, extremely sexy C.J., who had you all alone on his beautiful sailboat tonight. Is there anything you want to tell me, Jess?"

"Just that it was a fabulous evening. He did make

me panic a little by holding me a little too close when he brought me home. He was kissing me goodnight, but he apologized and said we'd talk about our future another time. I can hardly believe that God has brought such a wonderful person into my life."

"It is no secret what God can do!" Emily was singing the chorus of a song they'd sung in church last Sunday. Giggling, they both slid slowly down under the covers and were asleep in just a few minutes. What will their dreams be about tonight?

CHAPTER TWENTY

When Jessica awoke the next morning, something was ringing but it didn't sound like a phone or the alarm clock. She looked over at Emily's bed and saw that it had been made and there was no sign or sound of her in the house. She sat up on the side of the bed and then realized it had been the doorbell when it started chiming again.

Maybe she went out for the paper and locked herself out. She slipped into her robe and scampered toward the foyer. When she opened the door, though, she was shocked to see C.J. standing there. One look at her and a big smile was on his face as he greeted her.

"Wow, Sweetie, you look adorable in your half-closed robe, barefooted, and your hair all mussed up from sleeping." As she was trying to pull her robe closed, he caught her in his arms and gave her an unforgettable good morning kiss. "That boat ride must've really relaxed you or Em kept you up awfully late. She didn't look too wide awake when she got to work this morning, either."

"Wha...what are you doing here and why is Em at work already?" She glanced into the living room to see the clock. She turned back toward him with a red face and somewhat speechless for a few seconds. "I actually slept until 10 o'clock," she then muttered.

"Guess so," he chuckled.

"But why are you here, C.J., when I said I would take the whole weekend off if that would make you happy? Have you changed your mind and want to paint today?"

"No, but I thought we could do something fun together today and tomorrow if you don't sleep the whole weekend." He quickly entered the house and closed the door. It was as if he were continuing his advances of last night when he pulled her into his arms. He ran his fingers gently through her mussed-up hair and started kissing her neck below her ear as his wandering hands found their way inside her robe. Her pajamas covered her well, but she was shocked that he would do that.

"C....J....," she stammered as she felt his lips now inching slowly down the front of her neck. She was so surprised and upset that she couldn't find her voice, but her hands were suddenly on his chest. Pushing with all her strength, she backed him away. She couldn't hold back the tears as she screamed at him, "You get out of here right now, C.J., or I'll call the police, and I never want to see you again. You're no better than Todd." Sobbing, she ran to the bedroom and slammed the door.

He sat down on the couch, put his face in his hands, and tried to understand why he'd done such a thing. The experiences with those girls chasing him the last five years had some how flashed in his mind when he saw her standing in front of him in her untied robe, and he'd felt compelled to know if Jess was just another one of the same, just waiting for the right opportunity to make her move. *But, she hadn't known it was me at the door,* he scolded himself, *and I've been with her too many times now not to believe she is a true Christian, so why did I have to do this and probably lose another girl I was beginning to think I could truly love. How many chances will God give one guy to find his soul mate, anyway?* He'd lost all control of his emotions and had started crying.

Suddenly the sound of the bedroom door being opened startled him. He got up and hurried toward the front door. "Please don't go, C.J.," he heard her say just as he'd reached the door, and he turned to see her dressed and looking at him sadly but unafraid. "I need some answers and I need them now, before I pack my car and go back to Sanford. Would you please come into the living room so we can talk?"

He obediently went and sat back down on the couch where he had been sitting, hung his head and waited for her to lash out at him. He was really surprised when she came and sat down on the couch beside him, took his hand in hers, and asked, "Can you explain to me why you did that?"

"I honestly don't know, Jess," he sniffed and tried to keep the tears from coming back again, "but something snapped when I saw you in your unfastened robe. It took me back to the night I was asked to check something in a room but found this girl ready for you-know-what. No, that's not right. You wouldn't begin to know the things some girls will do to get a guy in bed with them, but it made me think that I had to see if you were for real, so I acted like a complete fool, Jess, and now I've probably lost you."

"The time I've spent being around you, C.J., has given me an insight into what true love is really like, and I realize now that I never did love Todd. As I told you last night, I'm excited to be with you and probably do love you very much, so I couldn't just walk away without knowing the reason for your rude actions this morning. The question is, what are we going to do about it? Do you want me to leave so you don't have to worry about who and what I am, do I stay and start the school without any communication between us, or do we try to remain good friends, learn more about each other, as we've been doing, and let the future take care of itself?"

"There's one more option, Jess," he grinned.

"And what is that?"

"We could get married real soon so I could have my sweet, adorable, lovable bride to shower with kisses and make love to instead of just dreaming about it every night." He then smiled that irresistible smile with the dimples in those dark suntanned cheeks.

"You were the one who insisted we get to know each other a lot better before we even thought about anything more serious, so what is this about marriage after my being here for only six days?"

"You've stripped me of all my defenses and I find myself completely under the spell of your charms?" he grinned.

"Well, we'll have to study that situation and try to find a remedy for it. I have a school to get ready to open so I have absolutely no time to commit to planning a wedding, right now at least," she giggled. "So what was the real reason for your coming and causing such a commotion this morning?"

"Oh, I was wondering if you'd like to drive down to Wrightsville Beach for lunch and then look around Wilmington this afternoon. Have you ever toured the North Carolina Battleship that's moored there? There're lots of other things to see, too. It's an interesting city."

"That sounds like fun. Let me check my make-up and brush my teeth and I'll be ready to go."

While she was in the bathroom, C.J. scooted to the kitchen, threw water in his face to wash away the tears, and got back just as she was coming out of the bedroom. "You look as fresh as a daisy, Jess. Shall we go?" he asked as he took her by the arm and headed for the door.

"Who's minding the store, so to speak?" she asked as they were soon driving south toward Wrightsville Beach.

"My assistant manager, of course. Oh, that's right, you haven't met Wayne Nilsson have you? He's been on a month's vacation to Sweden to visit his family, just dropped by the office this morning, so I put him to work. Maybe I shouldn't let you meet him, though. You might fall for that handsome Swede, and I'll end up a big loser yet."

His grin assured her that the Swede was either quite a bit older or he didn't think he would be her type, so she decided to play along. "You can't keep me from meeting another exciting Swede, C.J.. They are my favorite nationality with their sandy blonde hair, bright blue eyes, but sometimes brown, and a sparkling smile that sends shivers up my spine."

"You don't say? And just how many of these handsome Swedes have you met in your lifetime?"

"Um...let me see. One, two, three that I can remember," she answered with as straight a face as she could master.

He knew she was teasing him, but he continued to act the part of the jealous and upset boyfriend. "And just where were you fortunate enough to meet these handsome Swedes?"

"The first one I met was one time I was vacationing at a beach a little north of here, and the other two I met in Chapel Hill while I attended UNC," she related quite impressed with herself until she took a quick glance at him. She was disappointed to see him trying to keep from laughing, so she turned her head to look out the window.

"Did they ever invite you to their house for a meal so you could meet the rest of the family?" he tried to hold back the chuckle, but to no avail.

"They actually did, and I loved the whole family except for the younger brother. He turned out to be a little overbearing and bossy and also thought he could make advances on girls when he'd told them he was waiting for marriage."

"Is that so?" he said as he turned into the restaurant he'd picked to have lunch. He turned off the engine and reached over to pull her to him. "Will you admit right now that you were stretching some of that about the younger brother? I may have to leave you right here to find your own way home."

"And I thought you were a gentleman through and through. Oh well, I'll just have to call one of my other friends, or I could try hitchhiking. I'm sure I'd get home all right."

"I give up, Jessica Hale. Your wit and humor have outdone me, but only because I'm hungry and want to eat lunch. I guess you should be hungry, too, since you apparently haven't even had breakfast yet. Let's go. Maybe they'll be accommodating and fix you a breakfast plate." He was quickly around to open the door for her, kiss her on the cheek, and give her a big grin. "You haven't ruffled my feathers quite yet." He had gotten in the last word, after all.

CHAPTER TWENTY-ONE

The next couple of weeks kept them all busy as the Beachside was filled to capacity and they'd even called on Jess to help at the desk two or three times during the busy check-out time. She soon realized her business courses were a good basis for what had to be done but the actual implementation was learned on the job. She'd actually managed to do the tasks without causing any problems, and Em had been full of compliments for her ability to catch on so quickly.

The painting and cleaning were now completed and most of the furniture was in place so Jess was now working on the newspaper ad to get her students enrolled. She'd put an article in the paper earlier about a new school opening, but now she was stating the dates and hours for parents to come for a group session on what the school would do for the children and, in turn, the obligations of the parents.

Several parents had already dropped in to meet

her after Jackson and C.J. had put a beautifully detailed sign on the front of the building. One afternoon, she and Emily had gone into Wilmington to find a school supply store, and when they'd returned, there was the sign that Jackson had made himself, not to mention the tables that were delivered the day after they had declared the place spic and span and awaiting 48 little people she was so anxious to welcome into her world of learning.

She was hoping to have twelve in the morning class of 4 year olds, and twelve in the afternoon class held on Monday, Wednesday and Friday. On Tuesday and Thursday, there would be twelve in the morning class of 3 year olds, and also twelve in the afternoon class. She expected it to be a little tiring until she got used to the routine, but she was so excited that a miracle had actually happened in her life.

As she worked on the wording she wanted to put in the ad and the accompanying article, she was smiling as her thoughts drifted back to the day C.J. had taken her to the restaurant at Wrightsville Beach for lunch and then to Wilmington to browse around for awhile. They had toured the North Carolina Battleship and then driven around to see what the city was like since she and Em hadn't had time the day they'd come here. She and C.J., but maybe only she had, continued the rather sarcastic remarks at times until C.J. had finally pulled into a small park he was driving by. He'd gotten out without saying a word, and had just walked away.

She had continued to sit there, a little perplexed, for two or three minutes, until she couldn't stand the suspense any longer and had strolled over to where he was standing by a small pond. He didn't acknowledge her presence, and she had remained quiet as well. She had wanted him to express his thoughts first, but she was also thinking she had possibly carried her sarcasm a little too far which really wasn't like her.

At last, he spoke, "I love being with you, Jess, and I certainly enjoy listening to your quick wit and rather cocky attitude. I've been wondering, though, if you will ever be ready to consider a serious relationship with me, or are you thinking of me more as a big brother? You agree to do things with me, you seem to enjoy being with me, but is there any chance you are thinking of me romantically? When I mentioned marriage earlier today it appeared to me that you just brushed it off as a non-committal subject.

I was in love once before, you know, and I lost her. I didn't think I would ever find that kind of love again, but my feelings for you are becoming as deep, if not even deeper, than I had for Peggy. I don't know if I could take another loss, so I need to know where I stand with you before I lose my heart completely. Could you give me some kind of an answer, Jess, so I know how to proceed with my life?"

She'd felt so ashamed for the way she'd been treating him all afternoon, and she'd never given a thought about possibly losing him. She'd then had to stand there and hear him tell her where his mind had been while she'd been such a joker. She'd looked up at him and saw the torment in his eyes. She'd reached for his hand and brought it to her face so she could feel the love in his caress.

"I'm so sorry for the horrendous way I've been acting this afternoon, C.J., which is not normally me," she'd admitted humbly, "and now to listen to you tell me how you feel, it's incredible. I thought you had most likely seen the hero worship I didn't think I was hiding very well, but you need and deserve more than having to guess what is in my heart. The things I said to you earlier today, about experiencing what love is really like while I've been around you, isn't all you need to hear either." She'd turned to face him and smiled as she'd stretched her arms around his neck and pulled his head down so she could reach his lips. His reaction was swift and gratifying.

"You're the one I've been waiting for from the time I was about thirteen and had just started noticing that boys were different," she'd continued. "With only sisters, and being the youngest and the protected one, I was probably just a little slow in that most important category," she giggled.

"The dates I had before going off to college were mostly double dates, or groups of just good friends. So, when I met Todd and we started dating, I thought it was true love. I know now, though, that it was far from the real thing. So, I have to confess my experience is very limited, when it comes to dating and knowing what true feelings are supposed to be, but when you're around, C.J., my whole body feels things that I don't understand, and it's not just those silly, exciting tingles. I want to take care of you when you're tired, hold your head on my lap and let you sleep, make sure you have enough to eat, that you get to relax like on the boat, and all those things a person does when they love someone. And, yes, I do have romantic thoughts about you, but I didn't want you to ever think I was like those other girls you mentioned who were after you just because you owned a resort, not to mention you're one of the most handsome men in the world.

"The day Jackie told me about meeting her husband and loving him so much that she would've married him if he had lived in a hut; I knew that I could love you no matter what you did for a living. But, I wanted you to be the one to make the decisions, so I had to be a little stand-offish, didn't I?" She'd smiled as she'd again reached around his neck hoping for another of his kisses. He hadn't disappointed her, and then they'd sat on the ground for a little while watching the ducks that were enjoying the pond. On their way home, he'd asked her to use the center seatbelt so she would be closer to him. Of course, she'd been very happy to do that."

Now, as she returned to the present, she realized that the article for the paper was far from being done. She had been daydreaming for almost an hour, but when she got her mind back on the business she needed to take care of, everything seemed to fall into place easily and quickly. She was very satisfied with the results. *Maybe taking a little time for some day dreaming wasn't so bad after all.*

The open house was held the 16ᵗʰ of July, and Jess was thrilled with the response to her article in the newspaper. She had 25 children come with one or both of their parents for the 4 year old classes, and there were 20 for the 3 year old classes. She told them about the college courses she had taken, about her student teaching, and also some of the rules that were to be followed if they enrolled their child.

"The child is to be here on time and picked up on time. With two classes each day, I cannot be expected to baby sit, and school days will coincide with the public schools. And, another very important rule that I'll insist on, if and when you enroll your child, is that a picture be taken of the child with the person or persons authorized to pick up the child. The child will not be permitted to leave with anyone other than a person in the picture. This includes people the child may know, since that could be a father, mother, relative or friend who does not have custody or authority from you. This is for the child's protection as well as the parents and mine," she told them, "so do not send anyone else in your place unless you have made prior arrangements with me and I have a picture of that person. The police will be called in any other circumstance."

Enrollment dates were set with the 3rd of August being the last day they would be accepted. There were a few questions from the parents and then refreshments were served. They were also invited to look around the inside and outside of the school before they left.

Jessica felt things had gone well and several had approached her to say they intended to enroll their child and were pleased with the rules she had set forth.

CHAPTER TWENTY-TWO

When the registrations ended on August 3rd, Jessica was elated with the turn out. She had 26 enrolled for the 4 year old classes and 24 little 3 year olds. It had worked out the way she'd wanted with the 4 year olds, with 14 picking the morning class and 12 for the afternoon. She had discovered during her student teaching that an even number works much better for games, partners, and sharing books for reading. She was so happy she hadn't had to turn anyone away. She would now schedule private interviews with each family to learn things she needed to watch for, to take the picture that she had mentioned she would need, and any other information the parents and students wanted to share.

C.J. was as excited as Jessica, it would seem, as he came through the door with a big smile on that handsome face, pulled her out of her chair, and gave her the sweetest kiss she could've asked for. "Well?"

he asked as he studied all the papers on her desk. "Did you get the number you were hoping for?"

Grinning, she said, "Plus two! I have 14 in the morning class of 4 year olds. Oh, C.J. I'm so elated, surprised, and happy....I don't know what to say." So, she grabbed him around the neck, stood on tiptoe and kissed him. She had the oddest inclination to put her fingers inside his shirt, maybe unbutton each button slowly and lovingly so she could feel the bare chest she had definitely admired when they'd been on the beach in their swimsuits.

She felt her face getting hot just imagining it and tried to push away from him, but he was holding her too tightly. He tilted her face to look at her when he realized she was trying to get away and, of course, he saw her red face. "You are awfully cute when you're blushing, Sweetheart, but what made you turn so red this time? I've surely kissed you enough times, and you've also kissed me before, so what was so different about today?"

"Nothing," she giggled. "I was just thinking about something and it made me a little self conscience, that's all."

"Come on, Jess, tell me what it was. You haven't started keeping secrets from me, have you? Or have you?"

"I think we can have a few secrets, especially if they're embarrassing to the one who doesn't want to tell." She couldn't keep from laughing and her face felt even hotter.

C.J. picked her up and held her above his head like you would a little baby. "I'm not putting you down until you tell," he warned her as he started to twirl around.

"Your arms are going to get mighty tired, Mr. Peterson, because I don't want you to know what I was thinking I wanted to do to you."

"This is getting more interesting all the time. Come on, Sweetie, let me in on your secret." He had brought her down and tossed her over his shoulder like a sack of potatoes with her head dangling down his back. "Are you ready to give up and tell?"

But just at that moment, the front door opened and in walked Emily who had just finished her shift. "Well, I must say, you two are in a rather precarious position for such a distinguished resort owner and a very dignified teacher of youngsters," she laughed. "What in the world are you planning to do with her, C.J., or should I ask?"

"No, you shouldn't ask, Em," C.J. rebuked her jokingly as he put Jess back on her feet. "Actually, I was trying to make her tell me why she was blushing after she had kissed me, but I guess I'll never know now. What are you doing here, anyway?"

"Curious, just like you, Mr. Peterson. I wanted to know how the registration had ended up, and also to extend an invitation. Kevin wants to know if he can take us out to dinner either tonight or tomorrow night. And I'm asking if you might offer to take us for a boat ride afterwards. How about it, Boss?"

C.J. looked at Jessica and could still see some pink in her cheeks, but he thought he'd better get Emily answered, so he asked, "Do you have any secret plans you'd like to pursue tonight, Miss Hale, or would it meet with your approval to accept the invitation of Mr. Kevin Bradley for dinner and then cruise around the big pond out there?"

Nodding her head, she responded in the same manner as he had. "I believe that I would like to accept the invitation of Mr. Kevin Bradley for dinner, Mr. Peterson, but as for the cruise around the big pond, it must be with definite restrictions. There will be no rough play to get answers that are not willingly given, the hour of returning must be appropriate for working people, and we must definitely remember to keep our life jackets on at all times to avoid any accidents or those careless thoughts or actions." She tried not to blush but knew her face was turning red again as C.J. watched her with interest.

Emily sighed, "I don't know what's with you two, but it's very amusing to watch, I must say. I'll tell Kevin we'll meet him in the lobby at 6:30, if that's okay." They nodded, and after Emily learned the outcome of the registrations, she left.

"Keep our life jackets on to avoid any careless thoughts or actions?" C.J. reiterated her remark when Emily had closed the door. He reached for her but she dodged him, went into her office and realized immediately that had been the wrong place to go. His body seemed to fill the doorway as he leaned against the frame and had his legs crossed at the ankles, and his smile told her he knew he had her cornered. "What are you going to do now, Sweetheart, when I ask what you meant by those last remarks? Do they possibly have anything to do with the blushing you were doing earlier? Jess, you'd better tell me before my vivid imagination runs in a direction you'd rather it didn't.

Or maybe it was your own romantic thoughts that were wandering a little and that was the cause of the blushing." His eyes didn't leave her face but he had to start laughing when she attempted to cover her face with a paper she'd picked up from her desk. "Oh, my sweet innocent Jess; now let me think back to what we were doing when all this got started. You had just thrown your arms around my neck and kissed me, but you've done that before, so were you so excited that you were thinking about doing something else? We have to keep our life jackets on to avoid any careless actions, you said. Jessica Lee Hale, I do believe you were thinking some naughty but nice romantic thoughts. But, now, how do I entice you to follow through on those thoughts?"

"C.J.," she tried to keep a sober face but her giggles couldn't be restrained, "this type of conversation has to be stopped. We both need to get cleaned up for dinner and then take a nice boat ride." Her giggles wouldn't stop and when Jess giggles, C.J. can't stop himself from joining in.

"Okay," he got serious to a point at least, and

motioned for her to come to him. She shook her head negatively so he pushed himself up from leaning on the door frame and eased toward her. She moved on around the desk and thought she had a clear path to the door, but he was too fast for her. Pulling her into his arms, he tilted her chin and just looked into her beautiful blue eyes. "I hope you never ever change from being my blushing sweetheart, Jess." Giving a quick nibble to her bottom lip, he then covered her mouth with his and proceeded to kiss her with intense feelings.

All vacancies had disappeared again so Jessica had taken the room by the child care area of the resort when the pre-school registrations had started, but she usually spent the weekends at Emily's. She and C.J. had spent time on the boat and had also walked on the beach in the late evenings so they had learned a lot more about each other. She couldn't believe it had only been a little over four months since she had met him and Emily. So many things had happened and she had grown to love both of them. The Beachside continued to be full as early August was always the last chance for a quick vacation. It wouldn't be long until school would be starting, and vacations would be over until next summer for a lot of families.

C.J. had told her that they had been doing real well through October of the past few years, and they had some people regularly stopping all year on their way to or from farther south.

They all met in the lobby at 6:30 and Kevin had selected his own favorite seafood restaurant not far up the beach. Kevin drove his car so C.J. was free to tease Jess quietly in the back seat. He was really getting a kick out of causing her to blush, but then he had even continued after they were on the boat.

Jessica had finally had enough and went inside. She knew she had brought some of it on herself with her ridiculous thought of wanting to run her hands over his chest, but she felt it had somehow gone a little too far. It was about 15 minutes before C.J. came and sat down beside her. He put his arm around her shoulders, but she didn't move into his embrace as she had become accustomed to doing, and he slowly took his arm away and folded his hands in his lap.

"I've been a fool again, haven't I?" he asked. "I'm sorry, Jess, it's been so long since I've dated that I've forgotten some of the rules. You were so cute this afternoon that I didn't want it to end and proceeded to carry it too far. Will you please forgive me?"

"Do you think we could call it a night, C.J., or do Emily and Kevin want to sail for a while longer? This last day of registration has caught up with me, I'm afraid."

"Why don't you curl up on the couch or even crawl into the bed while I go and talk to them? I imagine they're about ready to call it a night, though." He lifted her legs onto the couch and put an afghan over her before leaving the cabin. The sails had taken them out a little farther than he had anticipated, so by the time they were back to the marina, everyone was ready to go home.

After explaining that Jess was rather worn out from meeting all the parents and students during the registration, Kevin and Emily thanked him for a wonderful boat ride, helped him get it docked, and then they left. He returned to the cabin to find Jessica sound asleep just where he'd left her. He hated to wake her after the long day she'd had, but he wondered if he could carry her to the bed in these tight quarters. He didn't want to take the bed and leave her to sleep on the couch, so he managed to get her settled on the bed and then crawled in beside her. He was sure it would only be a short nap.

We both have our clothes on, at least I have my shorts on, so surely it won't matter if we sleep for a little while beside each other, he reasoned. He'd taken his shirt off while they were sailing, and he wasn't sure he would even be able to sleep knowing she was beside him, but he suddenly felt tired and quickly slipped into slumber land.

He was awakened when he felt someone touching him. He found her still sleeping, but was amazed to discover her hand on his bare chest. Watching her, he saw her cute smile as her hand moved from one side to the other and then up toward his neck and started back down. He sure hoped she was dreaming of him because his hormones were really acting up, and he didn't want her doing this to anyone else even in her dreams. Her hand continued on down until it reached his waist and then stopped. He'd noticed tears coming from her closed eyes, and then he'd heard her softly whisper, "I'm sorry I couldn't unbutton your shirt." Now he knew what she was possibly thinking earlier at the school and why she'd remarked that the life jackets had to stay on. He just barely kept from taking her in his arms and kissing her.

Perhaps her own voice woke her, as she immediately sat up, bumped her head against the top of the bunk, quickly pulled her hand back to her side and stared at him. "How did this happen?" she asked as she was checking her clothes and realized she was still dressed. "I just remember being on the couch, so how did I get into the bed?"

After C.J. explained what had happened, they wondered how they were going to get to the resort without being seen this late. Kevin and Emily had left in Kevin's car so they'd have to walk.

C.J. checked his watch and realized it was 3 o'clock so very few people were likely to be out at this time. He'd pulled his shirt on, checked the marina and found all was quiet so they quickly got off and walked back to the Beachside. They lucked out as no one was out to see them, and C.J. went through the lobby to his apartment after using his key to let her enter the far side of the building next to the children's care center. She wasn't sure God would be listening to her after tonight, but she thanked Him anyway for saving her from a very embarrassing situation. She must've been overly tired because she was back asleep shortly after her head hit the pillow.

C.J. knelt beside his bed and apologized to God for his carelessness. He hadn't given any thought to how they would explain spending the night on the boat. He was, at the time, only concerned about making her comfortable. "Oh, Blessed Father, I wish we were married so I could spend my days and nights with her without worrying about how it would affect her reputation. I do love her, I want to constantly be near her, and I do thank You for bringing her into my life. Please help me to treasure her as a gift from You, protect her as I would my most precious possession, and forever love her with all my heart. Be near us, Dear Jesus, and guide us in the paths of righteousness."

Crawling into bed, he was soon asleep and dreaming of a soft, feminine hand softly caressing his chest. A big smile was on his face.

CHAPTER TWENTY-THREE

W alking along the beach the following evening, C.J. and Jess were holding hands and enjoying the breeze blowing in from the ocean. They were both engrossed with their own thoughts, but they had become used to the silence that enveloped them at times and were content to know that the other was near by. Jessica smiled as she'd glanced up and watched his sandy colored hair, that needed to be cut, being blown all directions; and he looked as if he were a pirate on the high seas. She wanted to stop and brush it back into place, but the wind was too strong for it to stay where she would put it. She sort of liked it mussed up anyway.

"Cameron, a penny for your thoughts," she said softly and then waited. Would he be alert enough to notice what she'd called him?

He stopped abruptly and turned to look at her. "What did you call me, Jessica Lee Hale? When and where did you discover my real name? Oh, I know, you're living with the Can't Keep Her Mouth Shut Emily, and she's told you all the family secrets, right? OK, out with it. How much more has she told you?"

She was giggling as she patted his cheek and stretched to kiss his chin. "You're a bit taller here on the beach, did you know that, Cameron. I truly love your name, both of them, in fact. Maybe, someday, if I'm really lucky, we'll have to think extra hard to find a name for our little boy that will go with James."

"What hasn't that girl told you?" He then suddenly grasped what she had just said. "Jessica, are you giving me the answer I've wanted to hear since we were in Wilmington that afternoon? Are you telling me that you *are* thinking of me in a romantic way and as a future husband? Are you willing to be romantically connected to me right now? Please let me in on your thoughts, Sweetie, and don't leave me in the dark." He picked her up and twirled around and around until he had them fall to the sand, side by side. A few guests were still on the beach and probably wondered what was going on with the two of them, but C.J. didn't mind as his lips found hers and he kissed her repeatedly. He then deepened the kiss and was thrilled when she responded as he had hoped.

Jessica had never felt so alive in her life, and she wished at that moment that they were married and she could experience all the love he had to give her.

C.J. still held her in his arms as they watched the stars twinkling in the sky and had both of them believing they were performing just for them. He finally turned on his side so he could look at her and then asked, "Jess, what were you really trying to tell me awhile ago? I know school is starting in just over a week, so please tell me what you're thinking. Do you know of someway we could squeeze a wedding in along with all your new school activities? That's all I've been dreaming about for the past month."

"The way you made me feel with those kisses, I wish we were married right now, but you're right, school is starting too soon. I had been sort of wondering earlier, with all your talk about a wedding, if we might possibly have a Christmas wedding. The vacation is a full two weeks this year, so we could get married the first day of vacation and have the full two weeks without *me* having to work anyway. Of course, that all depends on whether you're actually going to propose. I may just be dreaming."

He was immediately pulling her up from the sand and heading for the resort. "C.J., we have sand all over us," Jessica tried to convey to him as she struggled to stop him, but he was quickly inside the lobby and headed for his apartment. She didn't know what was going on as he pointed to the couch. "Stay right there," he said as he headed to his bed room. He was back in a flash, knelt down in front of her on his knees, and opened a small jewelry case which exposed a beautiful diamond ring. "Jess, my darling Jess, I can finally say that I love you with all my heart. Will you accept this ring as a token of my love for you and become my adorable wife over the Christmas holidays?"

"Oh...Oh...C.J., it's beautiful, but how did you have it tonight? You couldn't have known I'd almost throw myself at you out there on the beach and then practically beg you to propose to me. Why don't you think I'm like those other girls?"

"Because you're so different. I've learned to know you, Jess, and I've been the one who has been chasing you, not the other way around. I've loved you from the day I carried you in from the beach, although I wouldn't admit it. The first time I took you on the boat, I realized God had answered my prayers and you were the one for me, but I still refused to accept it. However, I bought the ring shortly after that because I had the feeling I would be needing it. I could hardly believe I was taking that big of a risk, but God seemed to be with me and He always knows what is right. Do you know the verse from Isaiah *41:13*? It says, 'I am the Lord, your God, who takes hold of your right hand and says to you, Do not fear, I will help you.' I have been relying on God to help me for awhile now and he brought you to me. So, My Darling, what is your answer?"

"Yes, Yes, Yes! Oh, I love you, I love you, I love you! I've dreamed about you so many times, almost every night, have daydreams about you, and every time you're close, my heart is beating like the little drummer boy playing."

"Just a little boy playing his drum? You disappoint

me, Jess. I thought I'd get a bigger reaction than that," he grinned.

"But he's such an important little boy, C.J.--he even has his own song that he plays and sings to the baby Jesus."

"I guess you're right, and I should be delighted that your heart beats like the little drummer boy's drum." She knew he was grinning, but as he took her hand and placed the ring on her finger, she was running her right hand through his mussed up hair that she had wanted to play with on the beach, and she knew the presence of the Lord was with them. It was breathtaking to feel the ring slipping onto her ring finger and to know that she could now call him her own.

"Has the little drummer boy's drum grown a little louder yet, Jessica Lee Hale, or can your heart only beat a certain speed where I'm concerned? I know mine is about to jump out of my chest now that I've finally taken the giant step to put my fears aside and accept the fact that God has given me the soul-mate I've been searching for so long. I had almost decided that I was going to be a loveless, wifeless, childless, and purposeless guy forever until I saw you needing me that day on the beach. Of course, I never dreamed, at that time, that it would end like this, but I'm so thankful you have come into my life, and I think we need to share a great big kiss to seal this engagement, don't you?"

"Oh, you make such wonderful speeches, C.J., and

I think my heart is doing a drum roll of the loudest kind right now and is heading for the crescendo with the big cymbals vibrating through my whole body. You have made me the happiest girl in the world, and I'm definitely ready to share that great big kiss with my hero."

He was laughing as he got up off his knees, but he was soon holding her in his arms and enjoying the great big kiss that gave them the security of a love-filled future.

CHAPTER TWENTY-FOUR

Jessica was trying to put the finishing touches on the school room, and she was continually amazed that Jackson seemed to read her thoughts or wishes as he kept showing up with things she needed for the school or to decorate with. He walked in one day not long ago carrying two small chairs, after he'd learned that she had enrolled two extra for the 4 year old class. Returning to the truck, he'd carried in a small table and placed the two chairs at the table. "For tea parties," he'd chuckled, "and also for little visitors you may have at times." She knew they were the answer to her dilemma of where the two extra would sit for their arts and crafts, learning their letters and numbers, and sometimes for reading.

Another day he came with several wooden animal plaques he'd cut out and painted which were exactly what she wanted for the rest room walls. He had also come with some trim, plywood and two large pieces of corkboard and proceeded to make two display areas for the students' art work. He explained, "You'll need one for the 4 year olds and one for the 3 year olds." Of course, they had fit perfectly between the three spaced windows on the long outside wall.

How did he know so much about what was needed, she'd wondered, and how much was he spending on all that he had supplied? So, the day he came with the extraordinary pieces of equipment for the outdoor area, she decided to ask him how he expected her to pay for all he had done. She'd wandered outside because her curiosity was getting the best of her about what he was up to now. She was in awe when she saw two five foot ladders, one each on opposite sides of a 4 sided platform and a slide beside each ladder. On the other two sides were entrances to two small tunnels, with peek holes along each side, going underneath the platform for the little ones, depending on their heights, to walk, stoop over or crawl, if they wanted, through to the other side and peeking out along the way.

The other was a platform about five feet off the ground with four ladders, one on each side. A wall was erected around the platform with two port holes on each side for spying on a friend or an enemy. Waterproof cushioned pads were installed below the port holes so little knees would not be bruised from the wooden floor.

Jessica was so impressed with the smoothly sanded and finished handrails, the steps and even the post supports. The sides of the slides where the children hold on were a tough plastic so there would be no splinters showing up with wear. She could only admire this man's outstanding work and love for the children's safety.

"Jackson," she finally approached him as she noticed he was gathering up his tools, "these are the most wonderful items and so beautifully detailed, but I don't know how I'll ever be able to pay you for all you're doing to help me get this school started."

He held his hand up for her to stop and listen. "Jessie," he said, "there is no reason for you to worry your sweet little head about this. I don't want a penny for what I've done and I'll tell you why. I was an elementary school teacher for quite a few years, and I also have a knack with woodworking that I learned from my grandfather, who was also a very prominent attorney. Well, besides the inheritance I received from him and my father, who was a professor, I won a substantial lottery a few years back. My wife and I had not been able to have children, so when she passed away six years ago, I was quite alone, or so I thought anyway.

"A very good friend had owned the Beachside Resort and I spent a lot of time there and also on his boat. When he wanted to retire, I helped him with the sale and some other details. I met C.J. during that time and he became the son I never had. I'd do anything for that boy, so when he came to me about this building and what it would be used for, I was elated. And when I met you, Jessie, it completed my joy to see your enthusiasm and your dedication to the job you were undertaking. It just makes me proud that I can be a part of it, and if I may, I'll continue to help whenever and wherever you need me. You have also become a member of my family, and I love you like you were my own daughter." His arms opened wide and she slipped in for a wonderful hug and a kiss on the cheek.

"Hey, what's going on here?" they heard someone ask as the door opened and C.J. came bounding out. "It's a good thing I came to tell Jess it was time to close up for the day. What have you been up to this time, Jackson, and why were you hugging and even kissing my girl?" he chuckled. Of course, he'd been looking at the slide and fort and he was like a little boy who couldn't help but run to inspect the brand new playthings.

Jackson smiled and winked at Jessica. As he watched C.J. checking every inch of the construction, he had to remark, "I just wish I'd known him when he was little." He bent down to gather up his tools and head into the building, muttering, "I should've put a gate in that fence so I didn't have to track through your clean room. I don't know why I replaced the section of fence I removed to get that equipment in before I got myself out. Maybe I'll get around to that gate one day soon." C.J. had caught up with him, took his tool chest from him, and carried it to the truck. The two stood talking for several minutes before Jackson slapped C.J. on the back, got into the truck and drove off.

Jessica had been watching from the window in her office, and it was so evident how much they cared for each other. C.J. came bounding back in and found her in her office just putting her purse over her shoulder. He took it back off and laid it on the desk as he wrapped his arms around her for the kiss he'd missed because Jackson had her tied up in that embrace when he'd arrived.

"You've made quite a hit with Jackson, you know that? He thinks of you now as his daughter, which makes us brother and sister. That means, if I know relationships, that we can't get married," he chuckled as his lips claimed hers for another long affectionate kiss.

"And that, Big Brother, wasn't a very brotherly kiss. But, isn't there something I can do to show Jackson how much I appreciate all he has done? Couldn't we at least take him out to dinner? It's so hard to know what to do for someone who has everything he wants."

"He loves the boat, Jess, and he's been out with me a good many times in the last five years. In fact, he showed me how to maneuver this particular boat. He'd been good friends with the owner of Beachside, and they'd spent many hours together out in the boat. When the owner decided to let it go with the sale of the Resort, I guess Jackson thought his days on the water were over until I asked if there was anyone who could show me the best way to handle my new toy. He jumped at the chance and became my instructor and my very dear friend.

The High School band usually has a concert around Thanksgiving, and Em and I have been inviting him to go along with us, which he seems to enjoy very much. So I think we can do some things that a father would enjoy doing with his children, and he'll be overjoyed," he chuckled.

C.J. saw the look on her face and guessed that she had ideas forming already about how Jackson could be included in the lives of the students. She would have 50 little ones very soon in this special building that Jackson had saved for just the right tenant. He was one great guy, and C.J. was so glad he had met him and now was able to give him the joy of seeing his building used for his first love--education.

Jessica had been keeping her parents and sisters informed about all the thrilling things that she had experienced while getting the school ready to open in just a few days now. Of course, they were overwhelmed with the generosity of Jackson and are anxiously looking forward to meeting him when they come down to visit. Unknown to Jessica, they had already made arrangements to come down for the second weekend of September. They'd drive down on Friday afternoon and return Monday morning. They had talked to Emily and then to C.J. asking that they keep it a secret from Jessica because they didn't want to interrupt her routine of teaching.

Talking to Jill one evening, Jessica had asked if T.J. had possibly told her about his ordeal with Adele. "Yes," Jill had responded, "he's told me about that as well as C.J.'s loss of Peggy. Those two have had all the tragedies they need in one lifetime. I went up to Chapel Hill for a weekend, stayed at his parents, and had a wonderful time. Did you get to see the Antique Store, Jess? It is simply unbelievable. I was so taken by it, I could have stayed for hours. I would actually love to work there and help people decorate their homes. It wouldn't be the real estate agency that I've dreamed about, but probably better in the long run and much more exciting.

And, I have another bit of news, Sis. Did you know that Dad has started referring to you as Jess? When Mom and I called him on it, he just smiled and said he sort of liked it. It had grown on him after hearing C.J. use it. How about that?"

"How many more miracles can this man make happen?" Jessica laughed. "Here's a story you'll like. I was talking to Jackson the other day, who is a miracle all by himself. He informed me that he has made both C.J. and me a part of his family, and he considers us his children. So, C.J. tells me we can't get married because we're now brother and sister." They both started giggling as they used to do when they'd shared their secrets growing up.

School was scheduled to begin on August 24, and Jessica was so excited she just couldn't believe she was getting any sleep. C.J. tried to keep her up late so she'd be tired, had her drink warm milk, and had finally bought some sleep medication to see if that would help. She'd only taken it one night because she'd slept until 10 o'clock the next day. She hadn't looked like she wasn't getting enough sleep and her energy was better than ever, or so it seemed. They got to wondering if she was only imagining she wasn't getting enough sleep so they gave up on all the sleep inducing ideas and things settled down.

The day arrived and everything went perfectly for a first day. She had studied the pictures until she knew each child and parent's name, the children were all well behaved, and she was giddy with excitement when the day was over. She wondered if their good behavior would last or had they all been doing their best to impress her the first day plus following their parents' instructions. Well, she was ready and wouldn't mind a few rowdy moments as they got to know each other.

The weeks passed quickly and she was so surprised when her mom and dad, Jill, and even Jodi and Rich had stood watching her little students leave about 3:30 on Friday afternoon. Just how everyone had kept that a secret from her, she'd never know, but she was so happy to see them. Jodi had put on a little weight but was still wearing her regular clothes. C.J. had invited Jackson to join them for dinner one night, and he'd told them he was thrilled to meet the family of his newly adopted daughter. They were all amazed by everything he had done at the school, and the ladies had to hug him before he left shortly after they'd finished eating. Stewart had to hold his hand and tell him he would always be welcome to come to Sanford and visit them.

It had been a wonderful weekend and before her family headed back home, they watched again as the little ones arrived on Monday morning. They all knew that God had been in on this exciting venture, and they each thanked Him in their own way.

CHAPTER TWENTY-FIVE

One Thursday in late September, Todd Olsen was sitting at his desk in his father's company, thinking back over the last four months. He had been examined and tested, had x-rays, MRI's, Cat Scans, seen both Psychiatrists and Psychologists, and in the end he had been declared physically fit and sane. Why had he acted like that toward Jessica, even to the point of taking one of his dad's guns and driving to Sanford? He didn't really have an answer except that he knew he'd wanted her so badly over spring break, and he'd thought being away by themselves, she would realize how much she wanted him, too. When she turned him down flat and had taken off during the night, it had done something to him.

"I still want her," he mumbled. "She's the only virgin I've ever known and I want her for my wife. I want to brag that I was able to marry an untouched woman."

He got up and walked over to his father's office. "Dad," he said, "could I talk to you for a few minutes?"

"Sure, Todd, come on in," his dad replied. "What's on your mind? Have you had a brainstorm for improving the company?" His dad's laugh was a hearty one, but Todd wasn't in the mood to appreciate it at the moment.

"No, sorry about that, but I was wondering if you'd mind if I took tomorrow off for a long weekend. I thought I might drive up to Williamsburg and look around. We haven't been up there for quite a while, and I'd just like to get away by myself."

His parents had been watching him like hawks and it was beginning to get to him. He wasn't a little kid anymore, and all the tests had shown he was normal, so why couldn't he take a trip by himself?

"Well, there isn't anything pressing on for tomorrow, so I guess if you want to drive up to Williamsburg for the weekend, it would be all right."

"Thanks, Dad, maybe I can dream up a new idea for the company while I'm there," he grinned as he turned and went back to his own office. He let out a sigh, and a smile was on his face as he sat at his desk and planned his weekend travels.

Of course, Todd's destination was not Williamsburg when he headed out that night. His dad had bought him a new car when he got out of the hospital and started working, so he knew Jessica wouldn't recognize it when he arrived in Big Breaker Beach. He'd had one of his good friends go to Sanford and check out where she might be. Pretending to be a college friend driving back to Chapel Hill from an interview for a job, he'd used the story that he'd thought he'd take Jessica to lunch if he could find her. Finally he'd hit pay dirt at a Quik Stop and discovered she'd opened a pre-school at Big Breaker Beach.

Todd had been a little surprised because she'd said she had never been there when they'd gone on spring break. *How had she made connections so quickly down there? And now that I think about it, who was that guy who got himself shot in the leg as he tried to save Jessica and her dad that day when I went to Sanford with the gun? She'd known him because she was on the ground beside him and crying instead of worrying a little bit about the handcuffs being put on me. A lot of things just don't add up, and I'm planning to get some answers this weekend.*

He got a room for two nights, and after grabbing a bite to eat at a nearby fast food restaurant, he drove around to see if he could find the school. *This is the hard part because I don't know whether she's teaching in a public school, one of those churches that have a pre-school, or if she found a rich old man who set her up on her own.* He had driven by the elementary school, several churches, and even the senior high school, but they didn't shed any light on what he was looking for. As he drove back along the beach, thinking he would have to wait until tomorrow because it was starting to get dark, he spotted the sign that was beautiful and even had a light to make it stand out at night. **Jessica's Pre-School**.

Yeah, it sure looks like someone with some money has latched on to her by helping with her dream, but has he also made her his possession? I really don't think she would compromise herself for the sake of the school she had dreamed of because she was so into that religion of hers. I even remember Dad talking to her and offering to help her get her pre-school started, but I ruined that when I acted so badly. I could've had her teaching in a school close to me and maybe even married to her by now. Why was I so stupid?

Well, I know my destination tomorrow now so I'll get a good night's rest and be ready to tackle the problem of conquering Jessica as I sit and watch the goings and the comings at the school. When she finishes her classes tomorrow afternoon, I'll suddenly appear and make her admit that she still cares for me.

Todd had an upsetting dream about Jessica not being there when he walked into the school and no one would tell him where she was. He just kept running from one end of the beach to the other, calling her name, but everyone was ignoring him. When he awoke, he was wet with sweat, his eyes were puffy and he was in a nasty mood. He'd have to do some calming down before he saw her, but he had several hours to do that. He showered, which helped a lot, and then he went to get a good breakfast with lots of hot black coffee. He finally began to feel like he was ready to tackle the task ahead.

A little before 11 o'clock he parked on a side street where he could watch the door, and he soon saw the parents coming to pick up their children. He was more interested, of course, in seeing the smile on Jessica's face as she gave each child a hug as she told them goodbye. Some parents shook her hand, some talked to her for a bit, and others actually gave her a hug.

She must be doing something right, he admitted as he admired the ease with which she had adjusted to teaching. Then she went back inside, the door was closed, and he again felt rather lost. He decided he would get some lunch and be back to watch the students arrive for the afternoon class. He actually took a short nap during the afternoon, but he didn't realize that someone had noticed the strange car sitting too close to the school and for too long. C.J. had his eye on that car, but it wasn't close enough for him to recognize the driver. Jessica had asked C.J. to go with her, before school had started, to talk to the police about possible periodic checks around the school because she wanted to be sure they would be available in the event of an attempted kidnapping or other emergency. They'd agreed they could do that, and also, it was agreed, if a call came in from her number, which was an extension of the Beachside, it would mean an emergency without her having to even talk to them. C.J. wasn't sure why they had missed this car sitting there most of the day unless they were using an unmarked car.

As always, at 3 o'clock, C.J.'s eyes were glued to the school door and watched as the parents drove up, collected their children, and left. His glance went to the car just as the door opened and he saw a familiar face emerge. He waited until he saw him crossing the street and heading for the door of the school. As he flew through the lobby, he called to Em, "Call 911 and tell them there's trouble at the school."

Jessica had gotten some thumb tacks from her desk and had just started putting up the pictures of little hands the children had drawn during finger painting. She had her back to the door so had just assumed it was C.J. when she heard the door open. She turned to greet him and had the Cee on her lips when she gasped, "Todd, what are you doing here?"

"Aren't you glad to see me, Jessica? Come here and let me show you how much I've missed you." He'd held out his arms as he walked toward her, but she was frozen in place.

"I'm just here to find the answers to some questions I've been puzzled about, so why don't you let me give you a hug, then we'll just relax and talk." He was almost to her when the door swung open and C.J. came running in.

"Stay away from her, Olsen," he ordered, but Todd quickly grabbed her and swung her around in front of him, like a shield. "So, that's the type you are, huh, hiding behind an innocent woman?" Holding up his empty hands, he continued, "I haven't got a gun to try to scare you with, so why don't you let go of Jessica and then we can talk like sensible human beings?"

"Who do you think you are, anyway? She's been my girlfriend for almost two years and we were supposed to get married. I just want to hear her say that she still loves me and we can continue our life together. Tell him, Jessica, just tell him that you still love me and want to be with me." He started twisting her arm, trying to make her talk, but she remained speechless. The only thing she could think of was how glad she was that her engagement ring was not on her finger. On finger painting days, she removes it so it won't get covered with the paint. The paint is washable, but she prefers to keep if off her treasured ring.

She finally cried, "Todd, you're hurting my arm. Please let me go so we can talk. We can sit down at the table and I'll try to answer your questions."

"Tell him to get out of here. It's none of his business what we talk about or do. I'm the one who loves you, and I want to get the answers I need from you." He started to push her toward her office while he screamed at C.J. to leave, but just then, the door opened and two officers entered with guns drawn.

"What's going on here?" one of them asked, and Todd immediately dropped his arms from her back.

"Oh, No....Oh, No.....Not again!" he moaned.

Jessica looked at C.J. with questioning in her eyes, so he spoke. "Officers, I had seen this strange car parked on the side street across from the school throughout the day, but I couldn't recognize the driver until he started toward the school a few minutes ago. He had caused Jessica problems before she came here, and I didn't think he was up to any good coming here today. I had my desk clerk call 911 while I ran over here to make sure he didn't hurt her until you could arrive. He has been through evaluations; at least his parents were to see that he was tested, so I'm not sure what the procedure should be now."

"Could I please get his parents on the phone and ask their advice?" Jessica asked as she looked at the officers, C.J., and even Todd. "I don't want to affect his future in his dad's company, but there has to be some way to keep him away from me."

"Don't you still love me, Jessica?" Todd whimpered. "I love you and want you for my wife. I'll do anything you ask if you'll only let me have you before you're touched by any other man."

The officers and C.J. looked at each other and shook their heads. "What do you mean, Todd, by your remark about being touched by any other man?" one of the officers asked.

"She's a virgin, and that is something rare these days. I've been with plenty of girls, but none of them were virgins. I want that experience."

"Is that the only reason you want Jessica to be your wife?" C.J. asked.

"Mostly, but she would be a good wife. She wouldn't need to teach, if she married me, because my dad pays me well. I really don't need to do much so I could spend a lot of time with her."

Jessica had slipped into her office to call Mr. Olsen at his office. He was definitely surprised to hear from her and distraught about Todd being there. He told her to tell the officers to hold him at the jail until he and his wife could drive down there. It would be between 2 and 3 hours.

She quickly returned to where the four were waiting and conveyed the message she had received from Mr. Olsen. She then knelt beside Todd, who was sitting in one of the little chairs that the students use, and spoke softly and calmly to him. "Todd, you asked me earlier if I still loved you. My answer to your question is that I've learned what I felt for you was not love at all, but instead, a result of my inexperience with dating and boys in general. Having grown up with my two sisters, and only group dating in high school, it didn't give me much insight into what real love meant, and so I assumed it was love when you paid attention to me and even took me to meet your parents. I enjoyed the time we spent together, and I do wish you a future full of happiness and fulfillment, but I cannot be a part of it. Can you accept that?"

"I guess I'll have to, but tell me one more thing. Who is this guy who always seems to be around when you need rescuing from me? Is he a guardian angel that your God has sent to watch over you?"

Glancing at C.J., Jessica couldn't control the smile that spread across her face. "I guess you could say that, Todd, because he has been there for me quite a few times now when I've needed him."

One of the officers stepped forward then, and taking Todd's arm, said, "Let's go now, Todd. We'll leave these people alone and go wait for your parents to come."

"I want to talk to Jessica again for just a minute," Todd said as he stood and pulled away from the officer.

Jessica nodded and walked over to him. "What is it, Todd?"

Whispering to keep the others from hearing, Todd said, "I just want you to know that I think I understand now why you had to run away that night, and I'm really sorry I acted the way I did. You've taught me a lesson about how to treat people I care for, and I think I'll look into learning more about this God of yours. I promise I won't bother you again so you can feel safe here at Big Breaker Beach. I also wish you the best with your school, Jessica. It's really nice."

And then, turning back to the officers, he seemed content to walk away with them to await his fate.

CHAPTER TWENTY-SIX

Octobre brought a variety of activities to the pre-school and Jessica was thrilled with the enthusiasm the little ones showed toward everything she'd presented to them. She had a lot of supplies from her student teaching so one day she showed them her colorful collection of autumn leaves. Sheets of paper with uncolored leaves were given to each child and then they tried to color theirs to match the samples lying on the table. All of them had mastered printing their first names now, so they got to exhibit their work with names, and Jessica loved seeing the excitement and pride in their eyes.

One Friday Jackson asked her if he could come and tell a story during the reading times on Monday and Tuesday. She readily agreed since he probably had lots of stories to tell from his teaching days. She was surprised, however, when he came to the door on Monday carrying a fairly large bamboo palm tree and also a miniature peach tree with a few peaches growing on it. He put them in the corner near the front window, spread a large mat on the floor and asked all the children to gather around so he could tell them a story. They quickly followed his instructions.

He then proceeded to tell them the story of Johnny Appleseed and the many trees that grew from the seeds he had planted across the United States. He passed around an acorn, the seed for the mighty oak, and showed other seeds he had from trees such as the maple. He also had a seed from an apple, a peach, and a cherry. "I don't think there are seeds that humans eat that actually grow trees," he told them. "However, the fruits that grow on trees are enjoyed by us every day. How many of you can tell me a fruit that grows on a tree?"

It was wonderful to see how many knew that apples, oranges, cherries, peaches, and even the banana grew on trees, and he displayed a real fruit when it was called out by one of the students. He continued by telling them about nut trees—the walnut, pecan, and almond, and he finished by giving them each an English walnut and a pecan, still in the shell, and their choice of a fruit to take home. He had shown them how nut shells are opened and the nutmeats taken out very carefully so not to break them, but he also stressed that it is quite hard to do, so don't be upset if they come out broken. It was a very interesting story time and the enthusiasm was very noticeable because everyone had been quiet and attentive.

When the children had gone outside to play, he picked up the trees and the mat to return them to his truck so he could carry them in again for the afternoon class. The palm tree was a gift to the school and remained in the corner of the room after he finished telling the story the second time that day.

The next day, for the 3 year olds, there was another bamboo palm brought in along with the miniature fruit tree. He set up this time toward the back corner where it got the light from the side windows. He didn't go into as much detail as he had the day before, but the children were just as enthused, and they also knew some of the fruits that come from trees. The room looked wonderful with the two live trees reaching out for the children to touch and learn to water and care for.

And then it was time for Halloween. The parents were invited to come and escort the children, if possible, as they paraded around a two-block area from the school; and who should show up as a very happy clown but Jackson. When they returned from their walk, Jackson entertained them with tricks which were plenty good to stump the little ones, but the parents caught on to his imperfections rather quickly. Yummy refreshments were then supplied by the Beachside Resort, and who would do the hosting other than C.J. in a real cowboy outfit, complete with a 10 gallon hat, a holster with plastic guns, boots with spurs, and of course, a mask. When he left, they all heard the Hi Yo Silver, Away!

Jessica had expected both Jackson and C.J. to beg off the next day, but they were there with as much enthusiasm as they'd had at the beginning.

On the 15th of November, when she'd brought the mail in, Jessica had noticed a personal letter that she expected to be from one of her family. She quickly glanced at the front of the envelope to see which one had written, but saw that it was postmarked Durham, and sure enough, there was Todd's return address. "What is he up to now?" she whispered as she placed the mail on her desk.

After the afternoon class had been dismissed and she had finished tidying up, she sat down to see what this unexpected letter contained. She was spellbound as she read:

> *Dear Jessica,*
>
> *I just wanted to let you know that I've found a church, like I mentioned that I thought I would, and I'm so happy to tell you that Jesus is in my life now and*

it has really made a difference. It was God's plan, I guess, that I meet you and be influenced by you to seek a new way of life. I've also met a wonderful girl, a lot like you, and I haven't even asked the question that had always consumed me. She is a Christian and that is all I need to know.

I hope you are happy, maybe with that nice, tall, handsome guardian angel who protected you so lovingly when I was such a fool. I hope the school continues to do well, my work with Dad is exciting, and I feel that I can contribute now that my life is really in the hands of God.

My parents are attending with me on Sundays, too, so we are truly a new family with a lot of wonderful things to look forward to. Thanks, Jessica, for the faith you showed me, and I remember you in my prayers each day.

Your once was lost but now am found friend,

Todd

Tears were welling up in her eyes when she looked up and saw C.J. standing there with a puzzled look on his face. She smiled and handed him the letter. "From Todd," was all she said as he took it and started reading.

"That is wonderful, Jess. I'm so glad he let you know that his life is on track now and God is at the helm. It is really a blessing to know that you helped a person see the way to change his life, but I'm sure you'll influence many more in your life time. Maybe you should frame that letter," he smiled as he handed it back to her.

"I may do that," she smiled back, "and set it right here on my desk so I can read it each and every day." She got out of her chair and went into his arms, saying, "Hold me, you handsome guardian angel, and promise you'll always be there for me as long as God gives you breath."

"I promise, Sweetheart," and he sealed it with a most wonderful kiss.

They stood embraced in each other's arms for a long time, it seemed, but then she tilted her head to look up at him with a sheepish grin, and asked, "Are you ready to help me cut out feathers?"

"Oh, goody, goody. It's almost Thanksgiving and we get to make Indian headbands for all the little Indians, right? When is the big day for the celebratory feast, this week or next?"

"Thank goodness, not until next Tuesday and Wednesday. There are 50 headbands to make and 200 feathers, at least, so my evenings are going to be full of cutting for the next few days. Are you game to help me? Maybe we can get Em to help us, too."

"Aren't you going to have some pilgrims with their white collars or those funny hats at least?"

"Yes, I already have those cut out, but I learned from student teaching that almost every child wants to make and take home a headband, so you have to be prepared."

"You are such a great teacher. I wish I'd had you for my teacher when I was just a four year old." He mussed up her hair and she gave him a little punch in the arm just to hear him whimper, which had become his habit.

"Could we go and get a snack?" she asked. "I'm really hungry, for some reason. Maybe it's thinking about Pilgrims and Indians and that wonderful Thanksgiving feast." Her giggles made him want to snuggle with her instead of eating, but she had grabbed his hand and was pulling him toward the door.

The following Tuesday and Wednesday were filled with giggles, screams, a few tears, but all around fun days. After they had made the feathery cuts to make them look like feathers, the students got to glue the feathers on their Indian headbands. Velcro was attached to the back so they could be adjusted to fit each head. Pilgrim caps were also assembled and then the collars and caps were worn by some of the girls who didn't want to be Indians.

Jessica had just started to read a story about the first Thanksgiving when the door opened and in walked Jackson with a live turkey in his arms. He put it down and of course that was when the screams and crying started. He picked it back up as he had it on a leash, and some of the boys came over to touch it after she finished the story.

They had been two great days except for dismissal time Wednesday afternoon. All but one of the parents had picked up their child when a strange car pulled up and a man Jessica didn't recognize came toward the school. She met him outside the door, but his voice got louder and more obscene until C.J. arrived and tried to make him stop it. The man had continued yelling, "I want my son and you have no right to keep me away from him," but just then another car arrived and the mother of the child, whom Jessica knew, came running toward them.

"I'm so sorry, Jessica. I was afraid he might try something like this over the holidays, and I had hoped to be here in plenty of time to avoid it. I tried to get away from the office a little early, but nothing ever goes the way I plan." Turning to the man, she said, "You know you don't have the authority to pick Danny up, and your visiting rights have even been taken away because of your actions last week. You had better leave now."

A police car had just pulled up to the front of

the school and the man took off running to his car. One of the patrolmen was able to stop him, however, and the handcuffs were put on. "I see you're still causing trouble, Dorsey. You'd think you'd learn after as many times you've been arrested. Come on, let's go find a nice hard cot for you to relax on." He then turned and smiled at the mother who was wringing her hands. "Court must've been a little heavy for you today, Irene, but I'm glad you were able to get here when you did. Hope you have a nice Thanksgiving. We'll see that this one gets a decent meal." Looking at C.J., he said, "We'll come for the car as soon as we get him settled down. Thanks for the call."

C.J. nodded and he and Jessica exchanged glances as she opened the door for Irene to go in and pick up her son. Before entering, however, Irene turned to C.J. and said, "I want to thank you, too, Mr. Peterson, for all you do to help Jessica here at the school, especially watching for things like this and calling the police."

Danny was used to waiting for his mother as she works as a court stenographer, and Jessica had agreed that he could stay with her, if need be, while she straightened up the room. He always wanted to help and did such a good job, it was a pleasure to help out this single mother. Danny had been busy today and had put almost everything away without supervision. He was a remarkable 4-year old and apparently had been trained not to come to the door. They were soon leaving with wishes for a Very

Happy Thanksgiving being exchanged and Jessica receiving a big hug from Danny. "I luv you a lot," he said softly to Jessica as he took his mother's hand and they were on their way.

"Another rescue, Mr. Peterson?" Jessica teased as she put her head against his chest and listened to his heart beating very steadily. "Are you getting so used to these episodes that they don't make your heart do double time anymore?"

"No, but I can calm down pretty quickly after the squad car arrives. Honestly, Jess, I didn't know a teacher had so many things to contend with or I may have been a little more hesitant about getting you a building," he grinned as he took her in his arms and felt so blessed that she was safe after another ordeal, and thanked God that he was close enough to watch over her.

They had struggled to find a plan on how to celebrate Thanksgiving as they both wanted to see their parents, but they also wanted to be together. A while back they had decided it would be best if they both drove to his parents on Wednesday and then she'd drive on down to Sanford Thursday morning. He would join her there Friday afternoon, and they would drive back to the beach sometime Saturday so she'd have time to get ready for school to start again on Monday. Hopefully they'd have time Sunday to spend some time together.

Their plans had changed several times, however, and he now asked, "Are your bags packed and are you about ready to hit the road?" She was unusually quiet and C.J. tilted her face to look at her. "What's going through that head of yours now, Jess? That look tells me you're thinking about something rather serious. Can you share with me?"

"I was just wondering about Jackson. What does he do on holidays?"

"I've asked him to go home with me a couple of times, but he says that the man who owned the Beachside lives in Jacksonville now and they always get together on the holiday. The band concert is next Friday night, however, and he has agreed to go with us then."

"Oh, that's wonderful, C.J. Well, I guess everything is under control then, and I'm ready for a big Thanksgiving dinner."

CHAPTER TWENTY-SEVEN

They found Emily and were soon on their way. They were to follow her, just for the holiday safety's sake, because Emily was used to driving the roads between the beach and Chapel Hill. She had done it quite a few times during the last five years. Also, she wasn't returning until Monday. Jessica was now riding with C.J. because he had suddenly decided they didn't need two cars. He would let her take his car on to Sanford tomorrow morning and T.J. would bring him down on Friday because he has a date with Jill. That way, they would get to be together on the road.

The time went so much faster, she realized, when you have someone to talk to, but C. J. seemed to be concentrating on a December wedding—theirs. "Do you have any idea, Jess, when we can work in a wedding and a honeymoon?" he asked. "I'll have to arrange for Wayne to be available, and also Em. She'll want to be at the wedding, of course, but I'm sure she'll get back as soon as she can, and I can trust her to see that things stay in tip top shape while I'm gone." He glanced at her to see if she was even listening to him since he'd heard no reply.

Finally, she spoke. "I was hoping to talk with Mom and Dad, and also Jill, tomorrow and Friday, but we'll have to check with the Pastor, too, to see if the church will be available at that time of year. We had mentioned the Friday before Christmas, but do you want to be away from home on Christmas Day?"

"As long as I'm with you, Sweetheart, it will be Christmas every day, so I don't mind being away from the rest of the family. I haven't been home every year because I had to be at the Beachside, but we did close for one Christmas so I could be home." He was smiling as he imagined how they might spend Christmas Day together, far away from their family and even their friends.

"You have a very intriguing look on that face of yours, C.J., so what's going on in that head of yours?" She was giggling as she was thinking of wonderful ways to spend a holiday in this man's arms.

"Oh, Jess, you don't want to know what's going through my thoughts right now. You may think I'm too consumed with romantic notions and decide not to marry me," he moaned.

"Um...I may be having some of the same, Mr. Peterson, and wishing that the next four weeks would go by extremely fast."

"Why, Jessica Hale, I do believe you've just

declared your desire to share a bed with me, and I'm ready whenever you like," he chuckled and then couldn't hold back a hearty laugh as he grabbed her hand and kissed the palm, the wrist and on up to the elbow. She pulled her arm away and remarked, "Keep you eyes on the road, C.J., so we can be sure to have a wedding."

"Yes, Ma'am," he retorted as he put both hands on the steering wheel and eyes ahead.

They talked about the difference in the scenery at Thanksgiving from when they'd both driven down in early June. The crops had all been harvested, the roadside flowers were almost gone, and the sky was more gray than blue today. "Do you think we may have a rain storm over the weekend?" she asked.

"I forgot to look at the forecast, but the sky sure looks like it could do something, doesn't it?"

When they pulled into the driveway at his parents, Jess immediately saw Jill's car or one just like it. "Is Jill here?" she asked as she almost jumped out of the car, but it was at that moment the front door of the house opened and her sister came running out to meet them.

"Yes, she is," C.J. chuckled as he watched the two sisters hugging each other and then heard Jess ask, "What are you doing here?"

"That's a story that I'm dying to tell you," Jill replied as she took Jess by the arm and led her to the house. They seemed to have forgotten poor C.J. who was left to carry in all the luggage, but T.J. pulled into the drive shortly, and the brothers got the job completed.

"So, you're going to have Jill close by and you can eliminate the drives between here and Sanford, huh?" C.J. nudged his big brother in the ribs and laughed. "If you've fallen as hard for Jill as I have for Jess, I think all the Hale sisters will be married soon."

"Are you suggesting that you and Jess have set a date? I hadn't thought you would be ready to make the commitment quite so soon."

"I think I've been ready to make a commitment to Jess from the day I carried her into my apartment from the beach. She is my life, T.J., and I thank God every day for bringing her to me. I was just existing, as you know, but that day became the first day of the rest of my life. So, definitely, I'm ready to make a life-time commitment to Jessica Lee Hale, and I'll wager that you'll be ready to commit to Jill very soon, now that you're going to have her around a lot more."

"You may be right, eventually, but for the time being I plan to take plenty of time to get to know her because there are a few things I just don't understand. She is certainly a lot different from those dates I was set up with during medical school. Not that I want any more of that kind. I've found myself actually fascinated, captivated, and I'm afraid, losing my heart to Jill, but I still can't bring myself to commit to her, or any girl, like I did Adele. I'm just having a hard time, however, keeping my hands where they belong."

"And you think you're not ready for marriage, Big Brother?" C.J. chuckled. "I'll just urge you to not continue living in the past, T.J., because a wonderful world and a great God await you to open up your heart again. You were the one, remember, who saved me from my wanting to commit suicide when Peggy died, and now I hope I can help you love again."

"Does Jessica know about Peggy?" T.J. hesitantly asked.

"Yes, T.J., she does. Em had opened her mouth and told her a little about us, but one night on the boat she remarked that I knew all about her and Todd, and now she'd like to hear about my past. I confessed all and she still assured me that she loved me."

Jill had dragged Jess up to the room they would share that night, pulled her down on the bed and then started crying. "I hardly know where to begin, Jess, but I'll start by telling you how happy I am that you met C.J. which has led to my meeting this wonderful family who has given me a new direction for my life. It's been sort of like a topsy-turvy Cinderella story where a small town girl meets a handsome prince who treats her like she is a lovely princess most of the time."

"What do you mean by most of the time, Jill, and why all the tears? You've never mentioned before that there were any serious problems between the two of you."

"I shouldn't have said that, I guess, but we're having a *little* problem that needs to be worked out. Anyway, he has made quite a few trips down home, as you know, and I've driven up here once or twice. What I want to tell you, though, is about one weekend, I stayed here for a game or maybe the special production the drama department put on at the college. I don't remember which one, but whichever, it was an outstanding game or performance and I had a wonderful evening. The next day, while T.J. and his dad were at the office, Mrs. Peterson asked if I'd like to go to the Antique Store with her, and of course, I jumped at the chance. Cameron Antiques really has quite a well-known reputation, you know, and I actually had goose bumps when we walked into the building. It is the most fabulous"....she stopped when she saw the most surprised look on her sister's face. "What's wrong, Jess?" she asked.

"Do you know what C.J. stands for?" Jess asked, but continued before Jill could give an opinion or an answer. "Cameron James, that's what, so it means C.J. was named after his mother's family. I can't believe he hasn't mentioned it."

"Wow, that's something else. However, to make my story short, Mrs. Peterson saw very quickly that I was interested in the store and asked if I'd consider working with her. She needs someone to help her with the financial part of the business as well as learning to work with the customers. I started to work part time about three weeks ago while I fulfilled my obligation to the bank, but we kept it a secret so I could surprise you when you came today. I'm staying here until I can find a place of my own," she grinned. "Of course, there's always the possibility of other arrangements being made, but that doesn't look too promising at the moment."

A knock on the door stopped their conversation, and they opened the door to find the two brothers standing there with a suitcase in C.J.'s hand and those matching grins on their faces. "Here's your suitcase, Jess, and are you two lovely ladies ready for some nourishment now? Mom has had some appetizers brought into the den and we've been asked to escort the two of you down there."

The rest of the evening was spent as a family, talking about the engagement and the forthcoming wedding, for one subject. Jess was so surprised how easily she was included in all the activities. C.J. hardly left her side, and she also noticed how attentive T.J. was to Jill. She couldn't get the remarks that Jill had made off her mind, however, nor could she forget the rare possibility that two sisters from a small town might find love with two handsome brothers from a somewhat different background. Jill never mentioned her tears or the odd remark again.

Jessica learned the next day that C.J. had known all along that Jill was going to be there, and that she'd be riding to Sanford with her sister instead of driving C.J.'s car. T.J. would ride down with C.J. and then go back with Jill since she will now be working at Cameron Antiques full time. It was so neat to hear C.J.'s name associated with the family business, and she's anxious to talk to him about it.

The drive to Sanford gave Jess a chance to tell Jill about the plans for the wedding and to ask if she would be able to help put some of the details together. They made a list of 'to do's' and figured they could get a lot of it done Friday before the guys arrived. Jill is to be her maid of honor, of course, so they could look for dresses, see the Pastor, and get a ring for C.J. They could leave the flowers and the reception for their mom to handle with just a little help from Jodi, maybe. With the baby coming in December, they weren't sure how much help she would or could be.

When they got home, her mom had to make a fuss over her beautiful ring, was also thrilled about the wedding plans, and assured them that she could handle the tasks they had asked her to do. It was to be a small informal wedding with mostly family and just a few close friends. When her mother asked about music, Jess told her she would get the soloist if her mom would ask the church organist if she would play about a 10 minute prelude of love songs, and the traditional Wedding March. Jess had an idea for the special music during the ceremony but wanted to be sure before she said anything.

They helped their mom get the meal on the table and the rest of the day was the usual Thanksgiving—too much delicious food to eat, the girls deciding to go for a walk to wear a little of it off, their dad snoozing in his favorite chair, and their mom curled up with a book. Jodi and Rich had gone home so she could rest and then they would go to his parents.

While Jill and Jess were walking, who should they run into but Pastor Steve out with his dog? Jessica asked if they could stop to see him in the morning, and he was curiously agreeable. "Do we have an occasion coming for which you need my services?" he asked as a big smile appeared on his face.

"Yes," Jess confessed, "and I know this time of year is a very busy one. But, as you probably know, I'm teaching now and Christmas vacation is the only time we would have for a honeymoon of any length unless we waited until next summer. We would very much like to get married on the Friday before Christmas so could we check your calendar as soon as possible to see if we can accomplish that?"

"An evening wedding, I presume. We do have a Christmas Eve service but there is nothing planned for Friday that I'm aware of. Do I happen to know the lucky guy or did you go and find a total stranger?" he chuckled.

"He's a total stranger to you, Pastor Steve, but a guardian angel to me in more ways than one.

He's saved me from possible abuse during spring break, from almost getting shot by the same boy, from another possible abuse attempt from the same boy, and from a father trying to abduct his child from the school. He has helped get my pre-school started, giving me his support, hard labor, and his love. I'm indebted to him, in love with him and don't think I could live without him," she smiled as she felt her face turning a brilliant red.

"He sounds like quite a man, but I'll never forget the fun those boys had at the youth meetings trying to make you blush, Jessica. I'm so glad you haven't outgrown that trait, and I hope your husband will enjoy and cherish your blushes for many, many years. Those were certainly some of the happiest years I've had in this church."

Jill was standing beside Jessica, grinning from ear to ear. "I've been told he's made her blush and loved it several times already. You have to admit that you couldn't ask for a much better recommendation than hers for a husband, now could you Pastor Steve?"

Chuckling, he said, "Maybe not, but I still would like to have a conference with the young man and you, Jessica. When will he be in Sanford so we can arrange that?"

"He and his brother are driving down from Chapel Hill tomorrow afternoon and then we'll drive back to the beach sometime Saturday. Would you possibly have time to see us on such short notice?"

"For you, Jessica, I'll try very hard to make room.

You drop by in the morning and we'll get the wedding date set, and then I'll check my calendar for when I can see you and your guardian angel. How about coming early in the morning, say between 8:30 and 9:00, before others start wanting my attention?"

"We'll be there. Thank you so much."

After they'd left the pastor, Jill remarked, "Jess, I know about Todd's first abuse, C.J.'s rescue, and the attempted shooting, but what are those others about?"

On the final leg of their walk, Jess told her sister about Todd's visit to the school, his letter about having Jesus in his life now, and about the father who tried to pick his son up from school yesterday afternoon. "C.J. has been there to help each time before the police arrived," she finished with a big grin on her face.

"You do have a guardian angel, Jess, and I'm so happy for you."

CHAPTER TWENTY-EIGHT

Friday was an exciting day for Jess and Jill as they had met with Pastor Steve and the church was reserved for a 7 o'clock ceremony on the Friday before Christmas. Pastor Steve had assured them that he would see that the organist was there to play the numbers Jess had requested, and he also promised to work with their mother so everything would be ready for the wedding ceremony. He had also checked his calendar for meeting with Jess and C.J., and had found some time around 4 o'clock this afternoon, 7:30 this evening, or 9:30 tomorrow morning for them to come. They would get it done someway.

They went to look at dresses next to see what they might find in a somewhat informal and yet exquisite gown for her wedding. The clerk showed them several styles that would've been appropriate, but they weren't exactly what Jess was looking for. And then she saw it, hanging by itself, and she was so afraid that it had been spoken for. She almost ran to it, and the closer she got, the more she knew it was the dress she had to have for her wedding. The clerk was smiling, when she joined her, and then explained that it had been received in a late afternoon delivery yesterday and hadn't been readied for display yet. "Would you like to try it on? It just happens to be your size."

"Oh, yes, please, I would love to try it on." Velcro closed the opening down the back for easy closing, but the flap had small covered buttons making it appear to be buttoned all the way down her back. Its high stand-up collar fit snugly around her neck and the bodice was perfectly tapered to just below the waist where it started to flare slightly as it went to mid calf in the front and dipped to floor length in the back. A light crinoline is included and can be worn to accent the flare, and the long fitted sleeves were Vee pointed at the wrist. She felt it had been made just for her. The headpiece that came with the dress was a small puff of veiling that just covered the eyes, was attached to a circlet of tiny roses, and a short veil continued in back and completed the look she'd wanted.

In the bridesmaid department they found a pretty velvet dress in forest green for Jill that was styled with a boat neckline and fit like a sheath with long sleeves and a hemline just below the knees. She looked adorable in it. Shoes to match were selected and all the other items she wanted for her honeymoon were found, too. Their shopping was complete except for a ring for C.J.

There were many more rings to choose from than she had expected, but she finally made her choice. Stopping for a late but leisurely lunch, it was almost 3 o'clock when they reached home. Their mom had just gotten home from the bank, and they needed to show her a picture of the gown and Jill's dress so she would be able to order flowers. She asked for suggestions of what they'd like and Jessica decided she would like deep red roses with lots of baby's breath and greenery. Jill thought she should carry roses, too, if that was what Jessica was going to carry, and they all thought ivory would go best with her green dress. The rest was left to their mother.

C.J. had called and left a message to let them know that they were running late. A sick child had apparently been brought to the clinic just before they were going to close at noon today, and T.J. was admitting him to the hospital for what appeared to be pneumonia. Jess called Pastor Steve and it was decided they would try for 7:30.

The guys didn't get there until 6:00 and were very apologetic, but it had given Jess time to talk with her mom about other details of the wedding, and the reservation was also made for the reception. A list for invitations was made for their family and friends, and Jess would get a list from C.J. and then see that they were sent.

After pizzas were ordered and devoured, Jess grabbed C.J.'s hand and led him off to the church for their meeting with Pastor Steve. They were going to meet T.J. and Jill later and go to a movie.

Pastor Steve was all smiles when he looked at the 6'2" solidly built young man that Jess came strolling in with. "Yes, I can surely see that you would make a very satisfactory guardian angel, C.J.," he chuckled as he held out his hand.

C.J. looked a little puzzled as he shook the pastor's hand, but when he glanced at Jess for an explanation, he only saw a blush covering her sweet face. He understood now that she'd given the pastor a vivid picture of his protective actions. "Just trying to protect the one I love, Sir."

"From what I've heard, you have done a very good job. I would've never thought Jess would have enemies wanting to hurt her."

"He wasn't an enemy, Sir. He just thought he owned her and got a little too possessive and caused her to fall right into my arms," he chuckled. "The other time it was a father who was thinking he could pick up his son from school but didn't have the authority to do so."

"Very interesting, but I guess we'd better get to the business of the evening. I have a few questions that I like to ask so I feel I know a little about both of you, your future plans, and your faith, and then I'll show you the rooms you will use before the ceremony, the Unity Candle stand, and explain your kneeling for prayer. The meeting had gone well, and C.J. was very impressed with Pastor Steve.

The rest of the evening with T.J. and Jill was fun, and after seeing how attentive and loving T.J. acted toward Jill, Jessica saw no reason for the remark Jill had made about T.J. treating her like a princess just most of the time. She decided to forget it.

Jess and Jill both packed a few more things in the cars Saturday morning while their dad had taken the boys to show them a few things of interest in the town and maybe get more acquainted with his future son-in-law. They were back in plenty of time to pick up the girls and meet Wendy for lunch after the bank had closed at noon. They then helped load Jill's car with the rest of the heavier items she'd wanted to take with her. It had been tearful again to tell their folks goodbye and to hug each other, but Jill and T.J. were soon on their way to Chapel Hill, and Jess and C.J. were on their way to Beachside Resort and the new life to which Jess is getting accustomed.

After getting a list of relatives and friends from C.J., he suggested she call his mother to be sure he hadn't missed anyone. Emily had told her about a small printing shop and she was able to get there on Tuesday. She got a wonderful layout and they promised to have them ready by Friday so she could get them addressed over the weekend, hopefully with a little help from C.J., and in the mail on Monday.

Signs of Christmas were everywhere and they were not missing in the classroom. On the 5th day of December, Jackson had come with a pre-lighted Christmas tree and during the following days, the children got to hang the ornaments they made and to put lots of tinsel on the branches. They were also kept busy coloring Christmas pictures, making Christmas cards for their parents, and also decorating their two palm trees with red bows. A Christmas story was read each day, some about the baby Jesus, some about Santa Claus, Rudolph the Red Nosed Reindeer, and The Night before Christmas. They also acted out the journey of Joseph and Mary with the donkey and being turned away at the Inn. They had the manger with a cradle and baby doll and they were the shepherds, Wise men, Joseph and Mary. Of course, it was Jackson who had built the front of the Inn, the Manger, and the cradle.

During the final full week of school before Christmas vacation was to begin, Jessica had a big surprise for all of them. She had six molds which she filled with Plaster of Paris, and while C.J. and Jackson supervised the other six or seven children on the playground, she had six per day per class making their hand print in a mold. A nub was at the top leaving a hole for a ribbon, and Jessica imprinted the child's name at the bottom because they still are making their letters too large to fit on the mold. Luckily, they dried enough between classes so she could remove them from the mold to finish drying and be ready for the next class. She had found boxes to put them in, and after a struggle to get them all wrapped, each child had a surprise Christmas present to put under the tree at home for their parents.

She was glad that she was kept busy because she would have been a nervous wreck otherwise thinking about the wedding coming up so quickly. C.J. had been surprisingly quiet and she got to wondering if he was having second thoughts about getting married so soon after meeting her. A week before the wedding, they were watching a movie in his apartment and she remarked, "C.J., you've been a little quiet lately. Are you sorry we're getting married this soon?"

He gasped and almost choked on a kernel of popcorn. "How could you even think that, Jess? I guess I have been a little quiet, but my mind's been on all the things I need to do before the big day. I wonder how you stay so calm with all the activities at the school as well as the wedding."

"I've delegated all my duties concerning the wedding to my mother," she grinned, "so I have all my time to devote to my students. Is there anything I can help you with to make it easier? Do you have your tux ordered? You **do** know that Mom is ordering all the flowers and getting the church and reception ready for us, don't you? Talk to me, C.J., is there anything I can do to help?"

Chuckling, he pulled her into his arms and snuggled. "No, Sweetheart, I really do have all that stuff taken care of. T.J. and I ordered our tuxes before we came to Sanford at Thanksgiving, I have your ring, and I have our honeymoon reservations. I do have Wayne lined up to be here, and Emily will be back the day after the wedding. There are only some personal things I need to get done, and you can't help with those." He kissed the top of her head and then tilted her chin to give her a long affectionate kiss. "It's just the waiting that's getting to me, if you must know. I love you so much I can hardly wait for our wedding day."

The next Monday and Tuesday, of course, Santa had to show up at the school for all four classes. A big red bag was over his shoulder and there was a present including a book, an apple, and a candy cane for each of the children. They came individually to get their gift as he took them from his bag and called their names that he had learned just like when he was teaching. Santa then told a story about his trip around the world in his sleigh, and that he always took Rudolph in case it was a foggy night in some of the countries. It was amazing how Jackson had been able to change his voice. The parents had been invited to come for Santa's visit and also to hear some songs and recitations. Refreshments of Christmas cookies and red punch were then served by some of the mothers. Now, Christmas vacation was starting and Jessica's wedding was only three days away.

CHAPTER TWENTY-NINE

As Jessica was putting the finishing touches on the pre-school before she left for her wedding and honeymoon, she was reflecting on her busy December. She smiled as she remembered the band concert they had attended the first Friday of December. Jackson, Em, and Kevin were in the back seat of C.J.'s car and with the two of them in the front, he had driven to the High School where the concert was to be held. The band had put on a most entertaining program that had them wondering how they could accomplish so much in a little over three months since school had started.

A week later, on a Saturday night, C.J. had bought four tickets for a Benefit Dinner Dance. Em and Kevin had other plans so he'd asked Jackie and her husband if they would come along. They were such an interesting couple adding to a great evening which had a few great speakers, even including a comedian, and the band had been great to dance to. She and C.J. had fit so well in each other's arms and had thoroughly enjoyed it, and just last Sunday night, they had all gone to the Children's Christmas Program at the church, which was so cute and she'd gotten to see several of her students up in front reciting a little verse or singing with a group.

And now, she'd finished checking her schoolroom and had it all locked up, so she was ready to see if C.J. was ready for the trip to Sanford to drop her off and then drive on to his folks in Chapel Hill. She found him in his office, leaning back in his chair, and of course, he had a contented smile on his face. Who could look anymore relaxed than that?

"Hello, Mr. Groom-to-be, are you going to wake up out of that dream so we can be on our way, or is the dream better than reality?"

"Hi, Sweetheart," he drawled as he brought the chair back to the upright position. Do you have a preference whether we eat here before we go, or stop somewhere along the way?"

She glanced at her watch and realized that it was already after 5:30 so she decided it would be better to eat before they left. C.J. picked the booth way back in the corner of the Deli so he could have more privacy, slipped in beside her instead of across from her, and then pulled her immediately into an embrace. "Just three days," he murmured as he slowly brought his lips to hers and lingered just long enough to make her want much more.

She couldn't quite remember whether they had

eaten or not, but they were now on the road heading for the wedding she'd been dreaming about for weeks. When he pulled into her parents' driveway, C.J. reached into the back seat and got a jewelry box which he presented to her. "With all my love, Darling, this is my wedding gift to you. I hope you like it and maybe you can wear it with your dress Friday evening."

She opened the box to find a delicate three-ruby pendant necklace set in gold, and a pair of dainty ruby earrings. She couldn't hold back her tears of joy. "How di-did you know my bo...bouquet was go.. going to be de...deep red ro..roses?" she stammered.

"You weren't supposed to ask that question, Sweetheart," he laughed, "but I called your mother because I didn't want the necklace to clash with the other colors you'd be wearing or carrying. I could've bought diamonds, but your mother thought you'd love the rubies. You aren't mad at me for doing that, are you?"

Jessica was laughing now at the idea she would be mad because he'd gone to all that trouble to be sure her colors would go together. She just scooted over to him, put her arms around his neck and gave him a nice long kiss. "Does that feel like I'm mad, you wonderful guy?"

They didn't want to part, but finally said goodnight promising they'd see each other at the church on Friday. Because of the distance, the parents had decided not to have the usual rehearsal dinner and instead shared the expense of the reception and the flowers.

Wednesday, Thursday and Friday would have dragged and been almost unbearable, but her mom had plenty of things for her to do. On Wednesday they picked up her and Jill's dresses and stopped at the flower shop. On Thursday they had gone to check on the buffet for the reception, the cake, and the decorations. Everything seemed to be in readiness. Of course, Friday was when they went to oversee the decorating of the church. It was beautiful. Red roses and baby's breath were entwined all through the candelabra, and a pretty vase of long-stemmed roses in red and white, along with baby's breath, was on a stand at each side of .the altar. The unity candle was encircled with small red rosebuds and the first twelve pews on both sides of the center aisle were adorned with a red rose tied with a gorgeous white bow. The white runner would be rolled onto the aisle before she made her entrance. C.J. had asked two of his fraternity brothers from Chapel Hill to be ushers.

When they returned from the church, she slipped into a wonderful tub bath, and felt so refreshed. Later, Jill came bursting into the room as Jessica was trying to fix her hair, but Jill, being more skilled in that area, took over. "The guys are already at the church," she said as she laughed, "and C.J. is pacing like he's going to the gallows. Are you sure you didn't dare him to go through with this wedding?"

"I'll never tell, but I'm glad to know that he didn't

turn tail and run," she giggled. "By the way, you haven't seen my wedding gift yet, Jill," as she opened the box to reveal the ruby necklace and earrings.

"Oh, Wow! Those are gorgeous. How'd he know you were carrying red roses?"

"He called Mom because he didn't want the necklace to clash with any colors I'd be wearing or carrying. Isn't that the sweetest?"

"He's one great guy, that's for sure, but I'm going to jump in the shower now and then we'll get ourselves over to the church. Just relax for a few minutes and I'll be right with you. Have you heard from your three sorority sisters who are to sing?"

"They'll be here." She had contacted the sorority and got in touch with the three girls who had been in the university choir and had sung together many times. They had promised to be there to sing The Lord's Prayer while she and C.J. are kneeling in prayer. She had informed the Pastor so he and the organist would know what was to happen, but nobody else knew except Jill.

It was finally time to go and she and Jill gave thumbs up to acknowledge that they approved of the other's appearance so far. Jodi had even popped in with the three-week old addition to their family, and his eyes seemed to be taking it all in. Jodi had also given her approval of the final touches to hair, makeup and nails.

Her dad looked so handsome in his tux, and his eyes were sparkling when he saw his two girls coming down the stairs. Arriving at the church, they were whisked away to the bride's room where their dresses were waiting for them. They didn't have long to wait before the prelude organ music began, and that meant in only ten minutes Jill would be walking down the aisle.

When the familiar wedding march was heard, Jessica found herself trembling, but it was with excitement, not fear. She couldn't take her eyes off C.J., and she wanted to run, not slowly walk to his side. Her father's arm was steady, however, and his smile so loving as he escorted her down the aisle and placed her hand in C. J.'s.

C.J. had watched in admiration as Jessica and her father had come down the long white covered aisle. How she could've gotten any prettier than he thought she already was surprised him, but there she was completely dazzling. Her gown was one of pure simplicity, but she made it fit for a queen. The necklace and earrings he'd given her were being worn, which truly pleased him. When she reached the altar, their eyes met and held in awe as the sorority sisters, unknown to Jess, had made arrangements with the organist to sing The Moment I Saw You when her hand was placed in C.J.'s.

Pastor Steve brought their thoughts back to the moment and the ceremony began. It wasn't long until their vows had been said, and as they knelt at the altar they were listening to the sorority sisters do a beautiful job singing The Lord's Prayer, a cappella. Jess was amazed that they got through lighting the Unity Candle without a fire, but the rings were finally exchanged, they were pronounced husband and wife, and C.J. had presented his wife with a most meaningful kiss.

The reception was spectacular, with a buffet filled with the most sumptuous food, and it didn't seem like there was an end to the people who had attended. She didn't realize she'd sent so many invitations as she kept meeting C.J.'s relatives. She was especially impressed with the Camerons, the sweetest couple who are, of course, Jeannette's parents and C.J.'s grandparents. There was quite a difference between them and the stalwart Peterson grandfather and his tall, lovely wife. They had tried to visit with everyone until someone came to inform them that it was time to cut their cake. They slowly moved to the table where the beautifully decorated cake, punch and coffee were waiting. A path seemed to open for them, and it was fun feeding each other a bite of cake and entwining their arms for a toast.

The band started playing and as they danced the first dance they motioned for some others to join them. After several dances together and also with their parents, C.J. whispered, "Honey, our plane leaves shortly after midnight, so we'll need to get started for the airport pretty soon. We need to load your luggage and change our clothes yet."

"OK," she whispered back, "I'll tell Mom and

Jill we're leaving and meet you at the door. My suitcase and clothes are at the house. Where are yours?"

"In the car. T.J. is going to take the things with him that I wore to the church, and I guess we'll leave your gown and my tux at your folks. I'll let T.J. know. Actually, I think he and Jill are together so I'll find Mom and Dad and see you shortly."

As their plane made its way from North Carolina to California, C.J. was getting more anxious every minute. He had been waiting so long for this day to come, and had taken quite a few cool showers the last two months. He chuckled, which caused Jessica to stir as she had fallen asleep leaning on his arm. He knew she was tired from all the plans and festivities of the wedding, and he was glad she could get some rest before they got to San Francisco. After all, he did intend to keep her awake a good while after they arrived. This was going to be an exciting experience for both of them.

He started wondering why he hadn't planned a honeymoon closer to home instead of clear across the country. They could've stayed in Raleigh, flown to a nearby town like Charlotte or Asheville, or even remained right there in Sanford. Now, that would've been quite a honeymoon. He grinned as he thought of the extra three hours that they're going to have because of the time zones, and he meant to put them to good use.

He hoped the other passengers weren't reading the anticipation in his eyes and his smile. He glanced at his sleeping beauty in the soft pink cashmere sweater and decided he'd be better off if he looked at the unromantic instruction book of the plane that was in the pocket in front of him.

Finally, they arrived at the hotel and were shown to their suite. Jess seemed wide awake now and had to see the view at night from their Bridal Suite windows on the 14th floor. She also thought she was hungry and thirsty so he checked the snacks and drinks that had been placed in the room. He didn't know if she was scared or was deliberately trying to kill him, but she was doing a pretty good job of the latter.

She only took a nibble or two of the snacks before she excused herself and went to the bedroom. A few minutes later, he followed and slipped out of his clothes and into his robe while she was in the bathroom.

When she emerged, she was wearing the cutest teddy that hid little of her body, and he knew he was ogling as she came toward him. He couldn't help chuckling, though, as she was blushing big time and looking at the floor instead of him. He opened his arms to accept her, whispered "Come here, Sweetheart," and she rushed to hide herself in his embrace.

As he pulled her tight against him, she could feel

his readiness through the thin, silky robe. *But we're married now, he's mine, and everything's okay.* All at once, she wanted to shove that robe off his shoulders and let it fall to the floor so she could see and touch the man she loves.

C.J. disrupted that thought when he whispered, "You look like a little angel in that, Jess, but I don't think you're going to be wearing it for long tonight. It's finally our wedding night and I get to show you just how much I love you."

She gave him a sexy smile and for an instant her thoughts flashed back to the fun she and Jill had that day picking out the lingerie items. It was the same day they had selected her wedding gown and Jill's dress, but now as C.J. sweeps her into his arms and carries her to the bed, she is running her fingers through his thick sandy-colored hair. She knows she is definitely ready to give and to receive all the love they have to share.

Her thoughts then turned to prayer in which she thanked God for his wonderful care and all the rewards she'd received for becoming a child of His when quite young. This night is the peak of the mountain she'd been dreaming for her life since finding her guardian angel.

ABOUT THE AUTHOR

While spending sixty-seven years living in Illinois, Sally had only read about the beautiful beaches along the eastern coast of our country. After the death of her first husband, she'd married J.T. Russell, and his children had lived in Virginia and the Carolinas for several years. On their visits, it was a thrill to finally see and walk on those beaches of North and South Carolina. As she was writing this story of Jessica and C.J., she could picture the places they had stayed, the boats they had watched, and the beaches they had walked.

She and J.T. left Galesburg, IL, to live in Charlotte, NC for over five years and then lived in Lawrence, KS for nine years until J.T. passed away. His son and daughter had both lived there for a time but are now again living in the southern states, and Sally has returned to Galesburg to be near her two sons and their families.

She will always have great memories of the trips they took to the Carolinas to visit and also for the weddings of the grandsons.

Printed in the United States
By Bookmasters